HIGH IRON

When the Pacific Northern Railroad hired Lonnigan to wipe out the deadly gang that held up their trains, they knew they had the toughest gun around. But what Lonnigan didn't know was that the job might cost him his life.

The brains behind the daring holdups was a man who had stopped at nothing. And now he planned his biggest haul—the theft of an entire train carrying one million dollars.

Lonnigan stood alone between a ruthless gang and a million dollar holdup.

Todhunter Ballard was born in Cleveland, Ohio. He was graduated with a Bachelor's degree from Wilmington College in Ohio, having majored in mechanical engineering. His early years were spent working as an engineer before he began writing fiction for the magazine market. As W. T. Ballard he was one of the regular contributors to *Black Mask Magazine* along with Dashiell Hammett and Erle Stanley Gardner. Although Ballard published his first Western story in *Cowboy Stories* in 1936, the same year he married Phoebe Dwiggins, it wasn't until *Two-Edged Vengeance* (1951) that he produced his first Western novel. Ballard later claimed that Phoebe, following their marriage, had co-written most of his fiction with him, and perhaps this explains, in part, his memorable female characters. Ballard's Golden Age as a Western author came in the 1950s and extended to the early 1970s. *Incident at Sun Mountain* (1952), *West of Quarantine* (1953), and *High Iron* (1953) are among his finest early historical titles, published by Houghton Mifflin. After numerous traditional Westerns for various publishers, Ballard returned to the historical novel in *Gold in California!* (1965) which earned him a Golden Spur Award from the Western Writers of America. It is a story set during the Gold Rush era of the 'Forty-Niners. However, an even more panoramic view of that same era is to be found in Ballard's *magnum opus*, *The Californian* (1971), with its contrasts between the *Californios* and the emigrant gold-seekers, and the building of a freight line to compete with Wells Fargo. It was in his historical fiction that Ballard made full use of his background in engineering combined with exhaustive historical research. However, these novels are also character-driven, gripping a reader from first page to last with their inherent drama and the spirit of adventure so true of those times.

HIGH IRON

Todhunter Ballard

GUNSMOKE

First published by Rich and Cowan

This hardback edition 2003
by Chivers Press
by arrangement with
Golden West Literary Agency

ISBN 0 7540 8210 5

British Library Cataloguing in Publication Data available.

Printed and bound in Great Britain by
BOOKCRAFT, Midsomer Norton, Somerset

ONE

IT WAS an Irishman, fresh from the peat bogs of the old country, who first called the Division Point the Top of the World. It was his tribute to the beauty of the mountains, and he must have had poetry in his soul, for the town could not have had a more appropriate name.

But the mapmakers of the Territory lacked his descriptive turn of phrase, for they carefully lettered in the name, Clear Water, and showed their opinion of the place by marking its location by the smallest black dot possible.

But to Randell Lonnigan as he rode his tired bay down Mountain Avenue just before full dark on this bleak, windy spring day, Clear Water was the most important town in the world.

It was the focal point, the nerve center from which the men who worked for the Pacific Northern Railroad operated the sprawling Mountain Division. It held the roundhouse, the tangled yards with their miles of passing tracks, the switchmen's shanties, the storage buildings, and the big station which on its upper floor housed the offices of the superintendent, the chief dispatcher and their numerous assistants.

Lonnigan stabled his horse at Chandler's Livery, asking the barn man to watch out for a buyer, then carrying his slicker-wrapped bedroll under one long arm, he moved out upon the slatted sidewalk, his eager gray eyes missing no detail of the town's busy main street.

His clothes were worn and travel-stained and not impressive to the clerk at Russ Pride's Mountain House. The clerk was new, fresh out of the East, come to the high country for his health, and he did not trouble to hide the distaste he felt for this small town.

He turned the dog-eared ledger and offered the snub-nosed pen and said, "Take number seven, cowboy," and reached down the key with a blue-veined hand.

Lonnigan sensed the man's contempt and his wide mouth straightened, but it was the first hotel he had ever been in in his life and he wanted no trouble. He scrawled

5

his name, and added after it Eagle Valley, and then he followed the clerk up the steps, walking with the short, choppy stride of a man who has been on a horse for a full day.

Two hours later, having freshened up and eaten at Ma Bellem's Railroad Rest, he traveled the length of Mountain Avenue, and with excitement rising, entered the station from the street side. There were half a dozen loafers in the dirty waiting room, their bodies sucking gratefully at the waves of heat thrust out into the stale air by the pot-bellied cast-iron stove.

Lonnigan paused, his nose quivering from the acrid coal smoke, and then, aften a moment's hesitation, he turned and mounted the scarred steps which led to the offices above, his high-heeled riding boots making a tapping sound on the hollow treads. He tried not to hurry, fighting down the tide of excitement which had turned him queasy at the pit of his stomach . . . it would never do to dash into the dispatcher's office.

Dix Dawson was on the key that night, handling the traffic from Indian Wells on the west to the endless plains which stretched out eastward toward St. Paul and Chicago. January was writing orders for him, and the call boy dozed in the far corner beside the stove, his knees supporting an open ancient magazine.

Lonnigan halted in the doorway, breathing deeply to school his eagerness, and then moved unobtrusively into the big room. He glanced at Dix Dawson's red head, bowed fiery and fierce under the cone of yellow light which fell on the open order book from the green-shaded hanging lamp. January's pen made scratching sounds across the tissue which blended with the uneven chatter of the sounder.

Lonnigan forced himself to wait, holding his flat-crowned hat in his big hands. Dawson was sending an order and did not bother to look up until he had finished and got his acknowledgment; then he raised his green eyes to Lonnigan's face.

"Help you?"

Despite his studied effiort Ran Lonnigan stammered with eagerness, but he managed to say fairly clearly, "I can use a job."

Dawson shrugged. Lonnigan was not the first cowboy to drop out of the high mountain parks, drawn to Clear

6

Water by the fascinating hope of going railroading. "Try the roundhouse or the trainmaster."

"On the key," said Lonnigan, recalling just in time how Uncle Charley had always said it.

"Oh." The dispatcher was surprised, but the instrument sounded as Smoky River reported Number Five in and out at nine-o-two. Dawson took time to mark his sheet before he asked, "Experience?"

Lonnigan flushed. It was the question he had been dreading, and only his heavy windburn hid his embarrassment. "I haven't any actual experience," he admitted slowly, trying not to stammer, "but Uncle Charley rigged a sounder from an old cigar box. He taught me the code before I was six, and we had a kind of game." This was harder to explain than he had expected. "We marked out a railroad on the bunkhouse floor. I used to send orders, Uncle Charley would set up problems . . . " His voice trailed off and there was silence in the big room, broken only by the clatter of the instrument.

Dix Dawson thought he was being kidded and he did not like it. "Uncle Charley," he said. "And who, may I ask, is Uncle Charley?"

"Was," said Lonnigan. "He died last week. He was a railroad man before he lost his leg, and he wanted me to be a railroad man. He raised me that way."

Dawson still wasn't certain that this was not one of Bullock's jokes. The superintendent was given to practical jokes when he had the leisure, but there was something about Lonnigan's steady gray eyes that forced Dawson to believe that this boy was telling the truth. And Dawson was a man of impulse. He had one now, and rose, indicating his seat. "Try it."

Lonnigan looked at him, then almost gingerly he slipped into the seat and touched the key. It was the first time in his life that he had even touched a real key. His fingers seemed a little stiff at first because he was uncertain.

"Send this," said Dawson, and scrawled an order to the Falling Leaf operator.

Lonnigan sent it. His first fumbling efforts were like a baby's diction in uttering a new word, but before he had finished the message he had gained confidence and had steadied into a rhythm.

Dawson left him on the key for the rest of the trick. He gave Lonnigan the schedules, the priorities, a full word picture of tho miles of twisting single mountain track.

7

And at the end of the trick he told Lonnigan to come back the next night, and then the next, and then the next. For two weeks there was no mention of a job, not even a promise, but Lonnigan responded as eagerly as if he had been offered the post of chief dispatcher. He learned, he steadied and he gained confidence. It was no harder, he felt, to run the Division than it had been to solve the problems set up by Uncle Charley on the scratched bunkhouse floor. He was entirely sure of himself, and then he met Paul Earnest.

TWO

Paul Earnest had learned his trade on the Pennsy, but he had been in the high country for the full three years since the construction crews had punched the Mountain Division through. And he was as suspicious as a good chief dispatcher should be.

He listened to Dawson and afterwards he stepped into the super's office on his way to take over his trick at the key.

"Dawson's having another pipe dream," he told Bullock. "Damnedst story I ever heard, something about a cowboy who trained on a sounder rigged from an old cigar box. Dawson's sold. He says the boy is a born railroad man, that he has coal dust in his eyes."

Bullock was busy and not paying too much attention. "What's the boy's name?"

"Lonnigan," said Earnest. "He wants to go railroading because an uncle of his named Charley was a railroader. I'm going to send him packing. It sounds like a made-up story to me. I'd guess that he's a boomer with a blot on his record who is trying to cover up with this fancy story."

Bullock put down his pen slowly. "Lonnigan," he was talking to himself, "Charley Lonnigan. I wonder." He looked at Earnest. "I used to work on the Reading with a Charley Lonnigan. We started as call boys. Better put this fellow on, and when you finish talking to him, send him in."

The corners of Earnest's thin mouth turned down. He was about to protest, but thinking better of it, he rose and went back into his own office. Lonnigan was hopefully waiting for him, standing politely beside the table.

Earnest measured him with a glance and what he saw did not alter his opinion. His years in the high country had not bred any love for the mountain people. They were too stiff-necked and unpredictable and, he felt, too unreliable to make good operators. Still, he had his orders, but he chose his own way to carry them out.

"I'm sending you to the Junction," he said. "You'll be

9

the night operator. The day man will tell you what to do. If you stick it out, you've got a job, but my guess is that you will quit."

Lonnigan flushed. He did not like Earnest and if it had been another type of job he would have put on his low-crowned hat and marched out of the door. But he wanted to be an operator, and if working for Earnest was the only way to become an operator, he would work for Earnest.

"Oh," said the chief dispatcher, not bothering to hide the fine line of his malice. "Bullock wants to see you, but don't think that you can escape going to the Junction by whining to him. You start at the Junction, or you don't start. Now, go on and tell him your troubles."

Lonnigan did not understand what Earnest meant, and he had no objection to starting at the Junction, but he went obediently down the hall and into the super's office.

THREE

Clyde Bullock was well named. He had powerful shoulders, a short, thick neck and a crop of heavy coarse black hair which his years on the Division had grizzled at the edges.

He returned Lonnigan's stare, but did not speak until the boy had crossed to his desk; then he asked abruptly, "Any relation to Charley Lonnigan who worked on the Reading?"

"He was my uncle." Lonnigan could not decide whether he liked Bullock's brusque manner or not.

"Good man, Charley." Bullock had picked up his burned-down pipe and was filling it, pressing the rough tobacco in with a broad thumb. "Did Charley suggest that you look me up?"

Lonnigan squirmed a little. "He said that when I was ready to go railroading you'd probably give me a job."

Bullock lighted the pipe before he growled through the smoke. "Then why didn't you come to see me instead of pussyfooting around Dix Dawson with that fool story? Earnest doesn't believe it."

Lonnigan's stammer was more pronounced and he flushed. "I always kind of figured that a man should get his own job."

"Fiddlesticks." To Lonnigan, Bullock sounded annoyed. Actually he was pleased. "Did Earnest put you on?"

A touch of pride crept into Lonnigan's voice. "Yes sir, at the Junction."

Bullock almost dropped his pipe, and his heavy face reddened with quick anger. He knew exactly what Earnest had in mind. Earnest was a sharp one. Earnest was obeying Bullock's orders. He was giving the boy a job, but by sending Lonnigan to the Junction he was telling Bullock that he resented the superintendent's interference in his department, and he was silently betting that Lonnigan would fail.

Bullock's jaws tightned and he leaned forward, studying Lonnigan with his slightly bulging eyes. "Tell me," his

11

tone was a thick-throated rumble, "are you afraid of ghosts?"

Lonnigan's eyes widened. He thought the superintendent was kidding; then something in Bullock's manner made him realize that this was not a joke and he shook his head slowly. "I wouldn't know." He was cautious. "I've never met one."

Bullock's chuckle sounded like the chuffing of an engine. That was the kind of answer Charley Lonnigan would have given him and Charley had been the stubbornest man alive. This boy, he thought, would do. This boy would make a fool out of Earnest yet.

"I'll tell you about the ghost," he said, and his bearded lips parted in a tiny smile. "The truth is that a bunch of hoodlums have been amusing themselves at the Junction by frightening our night operators. There doesn't seem to be any reason for the attacks. They've lasted nearly six months. Maybe it's drunken cowboys, or maybe it's some of Jim Koyner's men, working the meanness out of their systems. We've sent a couple of railroad detectives down there, but they left as rapidly as the other operators did. If it were any place else along the system I'd call in the law, but this division covers seven hundred miles of the roughest country God ever piled up on edge, and there's no law between here and Indian Wells."

Lonnigan nodded. He had been raised in the country. "But you mentioned a ghost."

Bullock shrugged. "Railroaders are a superstitious lot. About six months ago we had a holdup in the canyon east of the Junction. We think it was the Koyner gang, but we can't prove it. At any rate they wrecked the train. The operator at the Junction heard the crash and ran down the track. He tried to pull the engineman free and was scalded to death when the boiler went. His name was Chad Crawford.

"Well, ever since, whenever we don't have a night operator at the Junction someone breaks into the station and fiddles with the key, sending fake messages. Both Earnest and Dawson swear that it sounds like Crawford. They say they can tell by the way he handles the key. It's a lot of nonsense of course. I saw Crawford buried myself, but the ghost talk has spread all up and down the line until we can't get a man to stay at the Junction at night. We've been passing our trains either here or at Falling Leaf so it hasn't really hurt us too much."

Lonnigan was thinking aloud. "But why would anyone want to break into an empty station?"

Bullock shrugged. "Maybe it's some cowboy like you, who wants to practice being a telegrapher, or maybe it's some of your mountain people trying to cause the Road trouble. They don't like us, you know. They liked the country better before we built through."

"You mean Mars Jacoby?"

Bullock grunted. "You'd think a man like Jacoby would be glad to have the country opened up, what with the mines and ranches he owns."

"He's afraid of your land agents," said the boy. "He's afraid they'll bring in so many new settlers that he won't be able to control the vote any more."

"Stupid old hardhead." Bullock's face was red again. "It's about time some people came in here and brought some law with them. Jacoby not only doesn't bother the outlaws, he actually protects Jim Koyner. You know Koyner?"

"I've seen him." Lonnigan was cautious.

"Watch out for him," said Bullock. "Koyner's different from the ignorant bush jumpers that fill these hills. He comes from a good Boston family and he was involved in several confidence swindles before he came west. I can't understand why an educated man like Koyner goes bad, or why he prefers to live out in this wilderness."

Lonnigan didn't answer. He'd been raised in the mountains and he did not think of them as a wilderness.

"Well," said Bullock. "Now you know about the ghosts. The Junction isn't such a bad place to be. They even have some pretty girls. Ever meet Kate Jacoby?"

Lonnigan flushed. "I've seen her around at dances."

Bullock chuckled. "So help me, if I were ten years younger I'd go down there just to look at Miss Kate, but we aren't sending you up there courting. You're going up there to learn this business, and Earnest is betting that you'll quit."

Lonnigan started to say that he had no intention of quitting, but Bullock gave him no chance.

"I'm betting you won't," he said. "You're young, and you wear a gun. Keep your eyes open and use your head, and remember, both the railroad and I are depending on you to make a fool out of Earnest by sticking." He gave the boy a thick-palmed hand, and watched him go. Later he rose and walked heavily down the hall and into

13

the dispatcher's room. He drew his snap coin purse from his pocket, extracted a twenty-dollar gold piece and laid it silently on the edge of the table.

Earnest looked down at the coin. "What's that for?"

Bullock was grinning. "That says that you have made a fool of yourself," he said. "That bets that Lonnigan does not get run out of the Junction. If you have any gambling spirit you will cover it."

Earnest flushed. He pulled a handful of money from his pocket and tossed it down beside the twenty. "You're covered."

"That," Bullock told him, "will be the easiest bet I ever won." He turned and left the room, laughing.

FOUR

THE AFTERNOON mixed freight took Lonnigan down the long, twisting thirty-five miles of track, through Bright Canyon, across the raging White Water, over the hump and down through Paradise Canyon to the Junction.

Lonnigan was too new to railroading to realize that he was riding over the meanest piece of track in North America. The book said that the grades were only 4.2 but in places the book lied, and the tangents were enough to give a hardened engineman the shakes.

A dirty piece of iron, the track at times clung to the perilous shelf above the raging river, at others dived through cuts so narrow that they acted as perfect snow traps. They reached the top and sat on a mountain siding while the through sleeper banged east, its 1600-class engine fighting for time on the short straight-of-way against an almost impossible schedule. Then they crept back onto the main and felt their slow way westward with rights against no one. The train was a miscellaneous collection of battered equipment hauled by an old bell-stacker which leaked more steam than it ran into its pipes, but it was the first time Lonnigan had ever ridden on an employee's pass. He was a part of the road, everything was wonderful.

The train crew did their best to spoil his trip. They knew he was green, and they guessed why Earnest was exiling him to the Junction and they told with delight about how quickly the other night operators had departed. But, warned by Bullock, Lonnigan ignored them and they tired finally of the attempt at hazing and the talk in the smoky caboose turned to other things.

"This new Silk Express," the brakeman said. "It's a fool idea if you ask me." He was tall and thin and sandy, and his eyes were weak. He spat on the dirty floor at Lonnigan's feet. "Someone in Chicago must be out of their mind. What's the all-fired rush to send through a shipment of silk?"

The conductor was argumentative. "That shows you

15

don't know what you're talking about. The first silk to reach New York each season commands the top prices. In the old days clipper-ship captains used to race each other around the Horn to be the first ship in from China. Then they built the railroads through to San Francisco and the ships landed there and the silk was transshipped by rail.

"By the time Big Jim built this road, the Western and the Union had most of the freight business outside of our lumber. This Silk Express is a way to advertise the line. A ship from Japan is bringing silk into Seattle. As soon as it lands we're to rush it through to New York on better-than-passenger schedule. If we make it, everyone in the United States will be talking about the Pacific Northern."

"If?" The brakeman spat again. "But probably it will just break down and tie up the whole Mountain Division."

"What's it worth?" Lonnigan asked. "The silk, I mean?"

"Plenty." The conductor didn't really know. "Maybe a million dollars."

"Aren't they afraid someone will hold up the train?"

Both men turned to look at him. Both men laughed. "And what," the conductor asked, "would anyone do with a trainload of raw silk in the middle of the Rocky Mountains? Maybe you'd give it to Indians, or maybe Jim Koyner's outlaws could weave themselves some saddle blankets."

Lonnigan flushed. He was thankful that a moment later the old teakettle whistled for the Junction. Both the conductor and the brakeman rose and stepped out onto the rear platform.

The brakeman dropped off and ran back to set the switch, the conductor swung down and moved forward with Lonnigan following. He had been in the Junction before, but he had never seen the town from this angle and he was amazed at the size of the railroad yards, not knowing that future plans called for the completion of the cutoff, at which time the Division Headquarters were to be moved westward from Clear Water.

But the town itself was only a collection of some fifty buildings which struggled back from the main dirt street to climb in rising tiers against the sharp sides of the canyon walls.

The river made a wide loop, brawling around the yards in a thirty-foot-deep cut which curved to encircle the string of labor shanties at the lower end of the yard and then straightened to parallel the Junction's only thoroughfare.

But it was the station which held Lonnigan's interest. The yellow two-story building held the waiting room, the ticket office and on its upper floor the living quarters of the operators.

Below it, in a structure separate but connected to the station by a covered walkway, was the big lunchroom where the through passenger trains halted four times each day for thirty minutes while their hot and dusty riders gulped a quick meal.

The rear platform was long and narrow, between the switch track and the buildings. Ahead of Lonnigan the day agent appeared from the station with a sheaf of orders and walked toward the engineer who was already out with his long-snouted oil can, fussing lovingly around the wheezing boiler.

The brakeman had joined the conductor. Together they opened the front boxcar and a stripling in dungarees and a high-peaked Mexican straw hat appeared from the lunchroom kitchen, grasped the tongue of a hand truck and trundled it forward to the open boxcar, then, springing lightly to the truck bed, helped the crew who were already passing out dressed meat, sacked vegetables and contract pies. When the unloading was finished the stripling turned and Lonnigan was startled to see that it was a girl.

She jumped backward, lightly landing on the platform, almost bumping into Lonnigan. She swung, and for a long moment they stood motionless, staring into each other's eyes.

"Well," said Tracy McCable, and put her small hands on her hips above the sagging gun belt which she wore. "I hope you like what you see, Mr. Man."

Lonnigans' ears turned red with embarrassment. "I'm . . . I'm sorry." His stammer was very pronounced. "I was surprised. I . . . I didn't know you were a girl."

"Didn't you, now?" said Tracy McCable. "And what was it you took me for, a mountain lion?"

She was a small girl, coming hardly to Lonnigan's shoulder, and her red hair was tucked neatly under the hat until only a single stray curl escaped, and her face was a little thin, impishly intense and patterned with freckles. She wore a red-checked shirt and a thirty-two with a walnut stock hung easily in its worn leather holster.

Lonnigan was still hunting words. "I . . . I thought

17

you were a boy," he blurted. "In those pants, how could a man tell?"

Behind them the brakeman neighed with sudden laughter. "That's a good one, Trace. How can a man tell . . . ?"

All in one motion the small girl turned, her hand sweeping past her hip and bringing up the light gun. She fired twice as she came around, putting one bullet in the side of the boxcar only inches from the brakeman's head. The second cut between the conductor's legs where he still stood in the open doorway.

The conductor who had been laughing jumped convulsively. "Trace, take it easy. I've got three kids."

"I feel sorry for them," said Tracy McCable. "With a fool for a father." She turned back, her gun covering Lonnigan. "You laughing too?"

Lonnigan's mouth was open, but he was not laughing. He closed it slowly.

"Don't shoot him, Trace." It was the conductor. "He's the new night operator. Earnest sent him down to amuse the ghost. His name is Lonnigan."

"Hump." Tracy McCable stared Lonnigan up and down, then holstered her gun, and catching up the truck handle, dragged it toward the lunchroom door.

Lonnigan wiped his forehead, then turned as a voice said at his elbow, "You must be the new night man. I'm Dan Goodhue."

Lonnigan turned to find the day operator at his elbow and gratefully shook hands.

"Don't mind Trace," Goodhue told him. "The crews all rib her and naturally she has to fight back." He caught Lonnigan's bedroll and without further words turned and led the way to the station. After a moment's hesitation Lonnigan followed.

He came into the waiting room as Goodhue unlocked the door into the ticket office and then stood aside for Lonnigan to pass him. "They make them big where you come from."

Lonnigan had paused to look around the office and said, half absently, "I come from over in Eagle Valley." He walked slowly across to the table set in the bay window so that it commanded a view up and down the main line, and put out one finger to gingerly touch the key.

Goodhue watched him. "Whatever made you go railroading?"

Lonnigan turned. As always, when he had something

important to say he found it difficult to bring out the words without stammering. "Always wanted to," he managed. "Uncle Charley was a railroad man. Uncle Charley said that railroads were the greatest thing in the world."

"Well," Goodhue hid his quick smile, "I wouldn't go quite that far."

"They're useful," said Lonnigan. He knew that he sounded stubborn, but he could not help it. "What would any country do without them?"

"This country doesn't seem to like them." Goodhue glanced out at the wooded slopes which rose sharply on all sides of the small town.

"It will." Lonnigan was repeating words that Uncle Charley had used. "This country will grow. Men like Mars Jacoby and Jim Koyner can't keep it a wilderness forever."

Dan Goodhue looked at him. Long ago the day agent had decided that his narrow shoulders were not wide enough to carry the problems of the world. Once he had had this boy's enthusiasm, but, although he was well educated, he had failed at everything he had attempted in the business world and had turned to railroading because it seemed to offer a form of security.

Standing there he admitted that he envied Lonnigan his youthful eagerness, but at the same time he found that he was sorry for the boy. Life was a good teacher, but oftentimes a hard one, and, as he turned to lead the way up the stairs to the sleeping room above, he voiced his philosophy in a single sentence: "Don't take things too seriously, the railroad especially. It wasn't built in a day and it wasn't built by one man."

Lonnigan stared at him, not understanding, and Goodhue added, "Just do your job, boy, keep your head down, and life won't hurt you . . . too much."

He moved on up the stairs then with a puzzled Lonnigan following and led the way into the gabled bunkroom. Both bunks were stripped bare and Lonnigan hesitated.

"Take your choice," Goodhue told him. "I sleep at the hotel. It's more comfortable and I wouldn't stay in this building after dark for three times the salary the company pays Bullock."

Lonnigan looked at him and Goodhue saw the look. "You're thinking I'm afraid of the ghost?"

19

"Well . . . " the stammer was again pronounced. "I
. . . I . . . Bullock said . . . "

Goodhue looked at him thoughtfully, probingly, de-
ciding that Lonnigan was exactly what he seemed—a
green cowboy out of the hills.

"If Bullock told you about the ghost, why did he send
you here? They have no real need for a night operator
at the Junction."

Lonnigan flushed. "It wasn't Bullock. It was Earnest.
I . . . I don't think he liked me much. I think he thought
the ghost would run me out, that I'd quit."

"Yes," Goodhue agreed. "That's about the way Earnest
would do things, and if you want my advice, you'll do
just that, quit. There are other railroads, and other sec-
tions of the country where the people don't feel the way
the mountaineers do toward this line."

Lonnigan had been spreading out his blankets on the
lower bunk. He straightened, turned, and Goodhue noted
the long square line of his jaw. "I guess," he said slowly,
"that you mean well, but I'm staying. I guess that Uncle
Charley forgot to teach me how to run."

Suddenly Goodhue felt very tired. He said, almost
gently, "Loyalty is a fine thing. Maybe I haven't enough
of it, but I have reasons of my own for wanting to stay at
the Junction. They are more important to me than any
railroad, and in this country a man has to be careful. A
man can't stay here if Jim Koyner wants him to leave.
Bullock knows that, so does everyone on the railroad.
They do nothing about it, so why should I?"

He turned then and without further words disappeared
down the twisting stairs. Lonnigan stared after him, then
slowly he finished straightening his blankets and transferred his clean shirts to a drawer in the chest. Afterwards he followed Goodhue.

In the office below, Goodhue's manner had entirely
changed. Quickly he showed Lonnigan the routine of the
station, saying as he finished, "Actually there is nothing
for you to do. You can sit on the key and listen to the
traffic, report each train as it passes. Dawson will probably call you every hour just to make certain you are
awake." He pulled out his big hunting-case watch by its
leather thong. "Now go over to the lunchroom and eat.
Your trick starts in three quarters of an hour."

FIVE

THE LUNCHROOM was built in a triangle between the main track and the switch which ran out into the broad yards. Wide at the base, it narrowed to an apex which was only some six feet across. An L-shaped counter paralleled the two walls, giving a maximum of seating capacity, since the railroad was more concerned with the speed in which its passengers could be fed than it was with their comfort.

At the moment the room was empty and Lonnigan selected a seat at the center, directly opposite the kitchen door. He had no more than settled into place than the swinging door came open and Tracy McCable appeared.

She had changed from her Levis and now wore a plain checked dress, high at the collar, with leg-o'-mutton sleeves which puffed out at the shoulder. Her hair was soft and red, pulled back severely from her high forehead in a way that gave her a slightly pinched look, but the green eyes still showed their spark of devilment.

She stopped as she realized who it was, then came forward slowly. "So, it's the cowboy who wants to go railroading?"

Lonnigan had never felt easy with girls, but somehow Tracy didn't seem like a girl, she was more forthright. Maybe he was recalling the speed with which she had drawn the gun.

He grinned a little sheepishly. "Look, Sis, can't we be friendly?"

Her eyes frosted. "Don't call me Sis, and as for being friends, you won't be here that long."

Lonnigan's usually even temper slipped a little. "Wait just one minute." His long arm shot across the counter, and catching her small wrist, he dragged her toward him. "I'm getting just a little tired of being told that I'm going to run." His anger made him forget to stammer.

"Ha," said Tracy McCable. "A great big strong brave man. Did you come in here to eat or to wrestle?"

In spite of his quick flare of anger Lonnigan had to laugh. "Did anyone ever give you a spanking, Sis?"

21

"They did not," Tracy said, and jerked her wrist free. "We have steak."

"I'll take steak." Lonnigan was grinning. "You're quite a spitfire, Sis. Remind me. I'll give you that spanking when I have time."

Tracy McCable did not deign to answer. She turned instead and disappeared into the kitchen. Lonnigan sat staring at the slightly swinging door, speculating about her. She certainly couldn't be called beautiful, but she looked interesting. Someone, he thought, should put a rope on her, but she would take quite a bit of breaking.

The steak was good. It smoked in the middle of the thick platter, with a heaping mound of beans on one side, a helping of potatoes on the other. Lonnigan was hungry. In the excitement of the new job he had forgotten all about lunch. He was halfway through when the outer door banged inward and he turned to see Mars Jacoby coming through the entrance.

At first glance Mars Jacoby could easily have been overlooked in a crowd. He was short, standing barely five-feet-five in his high-heeled boots, but at second glance Lonnigan felt that anyone would sense that Jacoby had been born to command.

There was an arrogant vanity about the man. It showed in little things, in the extra-high crown of his hat, in his way of strutting like a bantam gamecock. Lonnigan had only heard vaguely of Napoleon and he did not notice the resemblance. He only knew that almost everyone in the mountain country fell somewhat under the influence of Mars Jacoby, that no rancher or miner in the district could hope to operate without Jacoby's blessing and that even Jim Koyner's outlaws, coming over from their Hole-in-the-Wall hideout, walked softly when Jacoby was around.

But it was the daughter who always impressed Lonnigan, increasing his natural tongue-tiedness. He had met her three times in his life and seen her not much oftener, but he shared the opinion of every rider in the hills that Kate Jacoby was the prettiest woman in the world.

She came in following her father, and Lonnigan's pulse quickened as she gave him a tiny smile of half-recognition. She was taller than her father by a good two inches and the well-tailored riding clothes made her seem more erectly proud than usual. Her face was oval, smooth, and there was a slight olive tinge beneath the clear skin which whispered of her mother's Spanish blood.

Kate Jacoby knew that she had seen Lonnigan somewhere, but she had not the slightest idea where, or who he was. Her father's memory was sharper, and he prided himself that he never forgot a face and seldom miscalled a name. He paused now, offering his hand, smiling his set, mechanical smile.

"You're Charley Lonnigan's boy from over Eagle Valley way. Heard about Charley's death. Too bad. What brings you to the Junction?"

"I'm working for the railroad." Lonnigan did not manage to mask all the pride from his voice. He was conscious that Kate's dark eyes were on him, although he did not dare look at her directly.

Jacoby's face hardened. His hatred of the railroad which, without his license, had invaded his preserve was well known, and he made no effort to hide his feelings; but before he could answer, the kitchen door burst open and a little man appeared.

He was no taller than Jacoby, and his body was thin and wiry. He had a big nose and the rugged irregular features which so often mark the Irishman. His face was long, his eyes blue, and a shock of stubborn gray-white hair stood up as if defying all the combs and brushes that were made. In his hand he carried a thick-bladed French knife which he was flourishing like a small sword.

"Mars," he bellowed, his brogue so thick that it was hard to understand, "I told you never to come here. I'll put ground glass in your food. I'll poison your coffee. Get out, you bloodsucker, living on the labor of other men."

Lonnigan's mouth opened slowly. Never in his whole life had he heard anyone dare to address Mars Jacoby in that tone. He started to duck sideways, fully expecting Jacoby to pull the heavy gun from his hip and blast this shouting midget.

But Jacoby's hand never moved. His voice was calm and filled with authority. "As usual, you are making a fool of yourself, McCable."

Instead of quieting him the words infuriated McCable to the point where he began dancing up and down, thrusting across the counter with his broad-bladed knife as if it had been a rapier. "You called me a thief," he

23

chanted. "You called Terrance McCable a thief, and you have the gall to show your ugly mug in my lunchroom."

"It isn't your lunchroom," Mars Jacoby's voice had tightened, "and you are a thief. I can prove that you sold three barrels of railroad sugar to my mine cook. Now, stop your caterwauling. Get back in your kitchen and do your woman's work. It's the only work you're fit for."

Lonnigan had risen from his stool, trying to avoid the knife. He was certain that McCable meant to drive the heavy blade into Mars Jacoby's chest and he half picked up his empty platter, meaning to use it to stop the infuriated Irishman. But to his amazement McCable quit, the knife in his hand sagging until its point rested on the smooth counter top, then with a choked curse he turned and scurried through the door into the kitchen.

Lonnigan stared after him open-mouthed. Slowly he replaced the platter on the counter and turned, feeling foolish as only a man who tries to stop a nonexistent fight can feel. Jacoby was paying no attention. He had turned as if nothing out of the ordinary had happened and was walking down the counter. But his daughter lingered for an instant, her dark yes smiling at Lonnigan, her soft lips forming a single word, *"Thanks."*

Lonnigan found that his hand was trembling as he brought out the half-dollar and laid it beside his soiled dishes; then he turned and hurriedly left the room.

SIX

THE STATION was quiet and all his. The work train from the new dam at the divide had pulled into the yards, its crew spreading out quickly, some of the tired laborers heading for their shanties, others toward the lights along the town's single street.

The night down-draft whistled through the twisting canyon, rattling the windows and bending the tree before it, and then a heavy lumber train, carrying Douglas fir out of the Northwest, beat its way over the switches and disappeared up the canyon, sending back echoes of its passage long after its tail lamps had faded from view.

Lonnigan had been sitting at the key listening to the traffic, picturing in his mind how he would execute each order that came over the wire. Most of his life had been spent at the little home ranch or in isolated line camps and he had never known what it was to be lonely, but for some reason the quiet station depressed him. He rose, moved around aimlessly, then paused behind the ticket window, studying the long green slips with their magic destinations printed in black ink. He hesitated for an instant, then lifted a ticket to Seattle from the rack and went through the motions of stamping it.

"Yes, Miss Jacoby," he said, speaking aloud to an imagined customer beyond the grilled window. "The train's on time. All our trains run on time. That will be thirty-four dollars and eight cents. Oh, a hundred dollars? Haven't you anything smaller?" He used the little key to unlock the cash drawer and began to count out change.

"And just what," said Tracy McCable, "do you think you are doing?"

He looked up, startled, his mind still engrossed with his imaginary ticket sale, then he flushed. "I never sold a ticket," he stammered. "I was kind of practicing."

Tracy moved to the connecting door and came in carrying a blackened coffeepot which she set on the stove. "And does Miss Kate Jacoby enjoy the trip you're giving her to Seattle?"

25

"Huh?" Lonnigan's flush had deepened.

"You're just like all men." Tracy sounded surprisingly bitter. "You never look inside a package. You just see the glossy wrapping."

Lonnigan tried dignity. "And what, may I ask, are you talking about?"

"You," said Tracy. "And Kate Jacoby. Oh, I watched you when she came into the lunchroom. You almost swallowed your tongue. I'll bet if Kate asked you to jump over a cliff you'd gladly break your fool neck."

"Miss Jacoby wouldn't do anything like that."

"Ha," said Tracy. "There speaks the ordinary male. There isn't a man in the Junction who hasn't jumped through hoops just for her smile, and they don't know her. She's cold and selfish and mean and . . . "

"Look," said Lonnigan desperately. "I never met anyone like you . . . "

"And you won't." Tracy was tart. "I'm unique."

"And Miss Kate is very beautiful and has always been nice . . . "

"That's your opinion."

"And just because Mars called your father a thief . . . "

Her hand darted toward her hip, but this time Lonnigan was too quick for her. His arms closed around her, pinioning them to her sides. For a moment they stood thus, the girl unable to move in Lonnigan's hold, Lonnigan afraid to release her. Her face was turned up to his, her eyes blazing, her mouth looking soft and red and invitingly parted.

Lonnigan kissed her. Never afterwards could be remember the impulse which prompted the kiss. He wasn't even thinking of kissing her. He didn't even like her, and then his mouth was against hers, and for a moment the tension had gone from Tracy's small body and she seemed to be straining against rather than away from him.

Then she tore herself free and without a word ran toward the waiting room, across it and out the door. Lonnigan went after her. He had some vague idea of catching her, of apologizing for the kiss, but as he pulled the door open a gun slammed in the darkness across the tracks.

Instinct made him jump backward, letting the door bang shut. He turned and raced back toward the ticket office, for the first thing that entered his mind was the possibility of a holdup. It did not occur to him until later

26

that Tracy might have fired the shot. All he could think of was the cash drawer which he had left unlocked.

But as he reached the ticket-office door the whole central window of the bay fell in, and a rock half the size of his head rolled across the floor coming to rest almost at his feet. He stopped, still in the half-shelter of the doorway, his eyes on the rock, for a piece of white paper was tied to it.

Gingerly he reached forward and scooped it up, pulling loose the string and straightening the paper to read in printed characters: LONNIGAN! WE DON'T LIKE MOUNTAIN PEOPLE WHO TURN TRAITOR AND JOIN THE RAILROAD. GET OUT OF THE JUNCTION AND STAY OUT UNLESS YOU WANT TO JOIN THE GHOST.

He head the note twice, puzzled by the use of his name. Only a few people in the Junction knew that he was at the station. And suddenly through his abstraction he heard his signal from the crackling instrument.

Without hesitation he crossed to the table, although it meant standing in full sight before the broken window. He answered and heard Dawson return: "Just checking. Seen anything of the ghost?"

Lonnigan's fingers trembled a little as he sent the answer. "Someone was just here. Maybe it was the ghost."

The unevenness of Dawson's sending showed his excitement. "You mean that the ghost was there? Did you see him? What did he do?"

Lonnigan thought a full minute before he sent the answer which was to become a part of the folklore of the Pacific Northern, to express confidence that no matter what the difficulties faced, they would be overcome.

"I didn't see him," Lonnigan tapped out slowly. "He threw a rock at me, but don't worry, everything is fine. He missed."

SEVEN

JIM KOYNER was waiting in the hotel lobby when Kate Jacoby returned from her dinner at the lunchroom. She had not expected him but she felt no surprise at his presence, for the outlaw leader came and went as he chose.

Nor was he alone, for she saw that Jocko Halleran and Indian Pete were taking their ease in the hotel chairs which faced on the big porch windows.

Koyner was not sitting. A restless man, he paced back and forth across the long room with the perfectly balanced movements of a cat.

He smiled as she came in, and she felt the little rush of excitement which she always experienced at sight of his lean, good-looking face. Here was danger. She recognized it by instinct, and welcomed it, and thrived upon it. She was a person who craved many things, but above all she yearned to be free of these mountains, to be released from the prison of her father's supervision.

James Koyner was not young. His thirtieth birthday was well behind him, and he had managed to crowd a great deal of living into those troubled years.

He had come into the mountains three years before, fleeing from an indictment in the East, and in those three years he had gathered about him the human dregs which had sought safety in the rugged land.

A natural leader, he had recognized that the mountains offiered a perfect base for operations. Every town in the district was a way station on the outlaw trail. This trail was not a single defined road, but rather a strip of country running from the Canadian border south to Mexico, through which men who were wanted by the law could travel with little fear from the Pinkertons or the detectives sent out by the large cattle associations.

In return for this security the brush jumpers respected the possessions of the inhabitants and conducted their thieving and their raids elsewhere.

This unholy alliance was an unwritten compact, fostered at times by the mine owners and ranches for their own protection, and Mars Jacoby had tolerated the wild bunch for years, recognizing perhaps that their aims and their morals were akin to his own.

But it was Jacoby's daughter who interested Koyner, for he realized almost at once that in Kate he had met a person as selfish and almost as ruthless as himself.

He was not unaffected by her beauty, but his interest was not primarily in her sex. He felt that she would make the perfect partner he had been searching for for years, and being experienced and well trained he had set about seducing her to his plans.

Nor had the operation been too difficult. At first Kate had been flattered, then intrigued and finally, when Koyner took her fully into his confidence, completely won over.

In Koyner she saw at once escape, a furthering of her ambitions, and a man who was strong enough to hold her straying interest.

She smiled now as she came forward quickly to give him both her hands. "I didn't expect you tonight. What happened?"

"Nothing," said Koyner. "Our man at Clear Water got us word that the railroad was sending down a new operator. We rode in to see that he does not stay."

"I saw him," said Kate. "Mrs. Bishop is sick, so Dad and I ate at the railroad lunchroom. A cowboy named Lonnigan. He won't bother you. He's green as grass."

Koyner shrugged. "We can't leave him here. The word is that the silk train will run sometime this week."

"This week." Kate Jacoby felt her muscles tighten with anticipation. "So soon." They had, it seemed to her, been waiting for years. Actually it was less than six months since the railroad had announced the running of the Silk Express and Koyner had conceived his idea.

"Are we ready?"

"We're ready," he said, his dark, oddly shaped eyes glowing a little. "We're more ready than the railroad— a lot more ready."

She laughed, a little gurgling sound deep in her throat, half excitement, half pure joy.

"So we can't have a night operator at the Junction."

A picture of Lonnigan rose before Kate's mind and she had an unprecedented feeling of compassion. "Don't hurt him, Jim."

29

Koyner looked at her, startled. In the three years of their acquaintance he had never known her to show consideration for anyone.

"Why?"

Kate Jacoby shook her head. For the life of her she couldn't have explained the impulse which had made her utter the words.

"I don't know. He's nothing but a boy. I used to see him around schoolhouse dances. He's a nephew of an old friend of Mars's from up in Eagle Valley."

"In love with him?" Koyner's tone was half teasing.

"You know better than that," she said. "You told me yourself that love is only for fools and weaklings. And I'm neither, thank you. But it isn't as if Lonnigan was a railroad detective or a Pinkerton man. He's mountain-born and his uncle had a lot of friends in this country. Some of them might not like it if he were hurt."

Koyner shrugged. "We won't hurt him. I'll send Indian Pete down to throw a couple of shots and heave a warning through the window. I'm not looking for trouble." He turned and called to the half-breed.

Indian Pete rose and padded forward, his moccasined feet making no sound on the wide boards, his beady black eyes fixed questioningly on Koyner's face.

Unconsciously Kate shuddered a little at sight of the breed. His clothes were greasy and unkempt. His black hair straggled down from under his broken hat, making a kind of frame for his narrow, scarred face.

The breed was a killer. He killed for the sheer love of destroying, and Kate had never seen him show the slightest emotion for anyone, yet he followed Jim Koyner like a well-trained dog.

Koyner gave his instructions quickly. He got a white piece of paper from the desk, printed the warning and handed it to the Indian who slipped from the room as quietly as an evil shadow.

Kate wrinkled her nose. "Whosh, he smells. I can't see how you stand having him around."

Jim Koyner's eyes glinted a little. "You can't always pick your friends by their odors," he said. "Pete's useful and he has no imagination. If I told him to hold up the Division Point single-handed he'd do it, and he'd probably bring me Bullock's scalp. How's your father?"

"Angry," said Kate. "He had another fight with Mc-

30

Cable down at the lunchroom. Sometime they're going to kill each other."

Koyner shrugged. "McCable's a thief," he said, "without having the grace to steal anything important. He doesn't take things because he's dishonest. He simply can't keep his fingers away from other people's property. Some people are like that."

"You?" she asked him.

Koyner looked at her. "Not me," he said. "I steal for the fun of it. I could have lived and died in my grandfather's house on Beacon Hill and probably made a thousand times more than I will ever make. It's fun to steal, Kate. It's fun to outthink honest men. It's fun to watch them squirm and curse and call down the law. I'm free, I do what I want, go where I please and take orders from no one."

"I wish I were."

"You will be," he promised. "Only a little while now and you will have all of Europe at your feet." He bent forward and kissed her, just as a single shot sounded from the direction of the railroad station.

"That will be Pete," he said, "persuading Lonnigan that he made a mistake ever to turn railroad man."

EIGHT

DAN GOODHUE was a man who appreciated his breakfast thoroughly. No matter how distracted the day agent was by other things he always managed to give full attention to what he considered the most important meal of the day.

The morning after Lonnigan's arrival was no exception. He ate slowly, deliberately the half-round of ham, the two eggs and the stack of medium-sized hot cakes. This, washed down by two cups of Mrs. Bishop's coffee, dissolved his morning sluggishness. The sluggishness was normal to him and intensified by his nightly habit of lingering long at the poker table in the rear of the Big Horn Saloon.

When Goodhue finished he lit his morning cigar and, strolling slowly, crossed the austere lobby and came out onto the roofed hotel gallery, and had his first look of the day at the Junction's main street.

He settled himself in one of the chairs at the far end of the porch, reflecting that as usual the street was not worth looking at. In the cold early morning light it lay littered and nearly deserted.

The swamper from the Big Horn made a small pocket of action as he limped through the saloon's flapping doors, carrying a bucket of smoking ashes which he dumped carelessly into the thick dust beyond the board sidewalk.

He had gone inside again when Jim Koyner, followed by Jocko Halleran and Indian Pete, banged open the hotel door behind Goodhue and, with never a glance in the station agent's direction, stomped down the steps and along the walk to the livery halfway down the block.

In five minutes they re-entered the street, mounted now, their horses made skittish by the night's rest and the cold air. They cantered along the street and took the upper road, disappearing around the twist of the canyon's mouth.

Goodhue watched them out of sight, his blue eyes half concealed beneath his sheltering lids, cool and calm and

32

reflective. Koyner, he thought, made a perfect figure of a man, lithe and quick, and handsome with his dark hair and his oddly shaped eyes. The eyes slanted a little as if the man's sailor ancestors had lingered too long on the China coast.

And Goodhue recognized the stamp of breeding in the man, and the carefully masked wildness which most people found intriguing, but his perception went further. Koyner, he felt, was unbalanced—not insane, but merely abnormal in his reactions and his point of view. There was never any telling what Koyner might do, and Goodhue always felt a distinct relief when he saw the outlaw ride away.

He turned his head in time to see one of the Italian women leave the labor crew's shantytown, cross the main tracks and come slowly up the street to Benson's store. Goodhue had no idea who she was. Her dark head was so muffled by a shawl that he doubted that her own husband could have recognized her.

And then the lobby door clicked and Dan Goodhue twisted around and had his reward for waiting. Kate Jacoby stood on the porch just outside the doorway. Her head was tilted away from him, so that Goodhue only saw her profile as she faced the watery sun which had climbed over the crest of the mountains to the east and was knifing its first weak rays through the thinish veil of morning mist.

Kate took no notice of Goodhue and he watched her with the motionless intentness of a faithful dog. She was entirely still, as rigid as a statue and as beautiful, the only movement about her the faint stirring of the wind as it touched the ends of her dark hair and whipped lightly at the fringe of her leather riding skirt. She stood thus for long seconds and then, catching Goodhue's watching eyes, she gave him a remote smile which held no welcome, but only tolerant recognition. Then she turned and stepped back into the hotel.

Dan Goodhue continued where he was, as if he could still see her image in the empty air. At last he rose and flipped his now tasteless cigar into the street and turned down the broad steps.

He was a man hopelessly in love, yet too clear-sighted to allow his emotion to blind him. He had studied Kate Jacoby until he knew her far better than the girl knew herself. He could read her thoughts and impulses and he

33

knew that as an individual he did not exist for her.

To her he was as impersonal and as sexless as the signal towers beside the railroad station; and as useful. If she ever had need of him she would not hesitate to call.

Months before, he had probed the depth of her selfishness and found it bottomless. Yet in spite of this knowledge he loved her, and no action she might take would ever alter his feeling. It was something utterly beyond the control of his reasoning mind.

Reason told him that she was not for him and that if she had been her greeds and weaknesses would have destroyed them both. Yet stronger than reason was a hope which was not even a hope, merely a wish, a nagging longing, a desperate need ...

"She's not for me." He spoke aloud. It was a habit which had grown on him in recent weeks. "She does not know I'm alive, and she never will, because I have nothing that she wants, nothing that she thinks she desires."

His measured steps had brought him opposite the Big Horn Saloon and he realized that he was still talking aloud and that the swamper was in the open doorway watching him with surprised, beady eyes.

He grinned at the man's look and moved on, then cursed under his breath. "I'll have to watch it," he muttered. "Everyone will decide that I'm crazy, and they'll probably be right. I am going crazy. She's driving me crazy. I'm insane to stay at the Junction. I'll leave today."

But he knew that he would not go. He had made the same promise to himself many times before as he waited on the hotel porch, hoping for a small glimpse of her face, for her remote smile which promised nothing and was, in fact, no deeper than the color on her lips.

Between these times he lived in hell, and he was honest enough to realize that it was a hell of his own making, for never by so much as the smallest sign had Kate Jacoby shown either interest in or curiosity about him.

He reached the railroad tracks and suddenly he remembered Lonnigan. At the Big Horn the night before he had heard a laughing reference to an attack on the new operator, but true to his policy of minding his own business he had done nothing about it.

He recalled now other mornings, other operators, hastily packed, waiting for the nine-o-five to take them east and he looked speculatively at the platform, half expecting to see Lonnigan's bedroll on the old boards. There was no sign of it and no sign of the night man inside the broken window of the bay.

Goodhue crossed the tracks and stepped into the waiting room, glancing around quickly for possible damage. He saw nothing and walked over to the ticket office, finding the connecting door unlocked.

He frowned. One of the railroad's strictest rules was that whenever the agent stepped outside, the office door must always be locked. He pushed it open and saw Lonnigan seated on the steps leading to the gabled room. The boy was cleaning a shotgun.

The reproof died on Dan Goodhue's lips and he asked instead, "Where'd you find that?"

Lonnigan had been busy with his oily rag and he did not look up. "In the corner of the baggage room. Someone sure let this Greening get into bad shape."

Dan Goodhue crossed over to hang his hat on the wall and replaced it with the green eyeshade which he habitually wore.

"What are you going to do with that?"

"Get me a ghost," said Lonnigan and looked up to give Goodhue a tiny smile. "Man with a forty-five hasn't got much chance unless he can see what he's shooting at. Shotgun is different. It scatters."

Goodhue hesitated. It was no part of his intention to take sides in this matter. He knew, as did almost everyone in the Junction, that the attacks on the night operators had been carried out by Jim Koyner's men and he was still puzzled by the motive which would make Koyner ride miles out of his way simply to run a new operator out of the station.

Most of the town had long since ceased to worry about Koyner's motive. To them it had become a kind of game, and since on principle they disliked both the railroad and railroad men, they welcomed the atacks since they furnished a new subject for conversation, a means of breaking the slow, creeping boredom of the place.

But looking at Lonnigan, Goodhue found himself moved by an impulse which was disturbing. There was something very likable and unassuming about the boy. And it was so very obvious how much importance he attached to holding this job.

"I'm going to give you a word of advice," Goodhue

35

said. "I could have told you last night but you wouldn't have listened then. Maybe you won't listen today, but you should, for your own good. Forget the shotgun. Get on the nine-o-five and go back to Clear Water and shove this job between Earnest's teeth."

"I do not have any attention of being run out."

"Some of the other operators felt the same way," Goodhue told him. "One was a railroad detective and very tough. They beat the hell out of him and dumped him unconscious onto a westbound freight. He didn't come to until he hit the Seattle yards."

Lonnigan was still polishing the gun. "They've got to get close enough to beat me," he said. "I loosened one of the upstairs windows so I can climb up to the roof. From there I can get me a couple of ghosts. You wouldn't know why they are doing this?"

Goodhue said honestly, "I wouldn't tell you if I did. The railroad pays me a hundred and ten dollars a month. For that I work twelve hours, I make out waybills, I sell a few tickets, I act as baggageman and freight agent. I am not a railroad detective and if I make any guesses I keep them to myself."

Lonnigan looked at him, then he rose easily and placed the gun in the corner.

"And if you make any guesses," Goodhue added, "you'll be smart if you follow my example. Now, go get your breakfast."

He watched the boy go, and then feeling dissatisfied, turned and examined the broken window.

NINE

IT WAS AFTER eight when Lonnigan ducked his head and stepped through the lunchroom entrance. The room was empty save for the crew of the work train who were just finishing their morning meal. They rose, the engineman in the lead, and moved past Lonnigan toward the door, joking among themselves as they went. At the entrance the engineer paused and said in an extra-large voice, "I see we still got a night operator."

"We won't have him tomorrow," the labor foreman said and, chuckling, followed the engineman from the building.

Lonnigan glared after them, his fists tightening at his sides, then turned to find that Tracy McCable had come through the swinging door and was regarding him from the far side of the counter.

He sat down, wrapping his long legs around the spindle of the stool and shoving his flat hat far back on his head. "Sis," he said, "I don't get it. Here are a lot of men drawing the railroad's pay and they act like they think it's a joke that someone is busting railroad windows and running off operators." He sounded genuinely puzzled.

"That is because you are not overly bright," said Tracy McCable.

Lonnigan scuffed at the side of his chin with the heel of his hand. "Could be." He gave her a small grin. "Uncle Charley always said a man didn't have to be so all-fired smart if he learned the right habits early. Now, I always learned that you were loyal to your brand. If you were riding for an outfit you watched out for the outfit's interests. Why's it different on a railroad?"

"It's not."

"Sis," he said, "I just don't understand."

Tracy McCable shook her small red head. "Men are as stupid as sheep," she told him. "They like to follow a leader. In the Junction it is downright popular to take slams at the railroad. Mars Jacoby does it. Jim Koyner

37

does it. Even the workers who draw their pay from the railroad do it—if they have to live here."

Lonnigan squinted at her. "You know, those freckles are kind of deceptive. They make you look kind of dumb, and I think maybe they are right."

"You," said Tracy with dignity, "are the wrongest person I have listened to in some while. Behind these freckles I have probably got the shrewdest brain in these whole mountains."

"Do tell?"

"I am telling you for your own good."

Lonnigan's eyes got a sleepy look. Had Tracy known him better she would have realized that this was what Uncle Charley had always called Lonnigan's studying look. It was the same that Ran used in a poker game when he did not wish the other players to know what he was thinking.

"If you've got such a good brain," he said slowly, "answer me one question. Why is someone so concerned with running the night operators away from the Junction?"

"Ha," said Tracy. "Then men who operate this railroad think it is just a kind of game."

"Is that what you think?"

"I . . . am too smart to think about things that are not my business."

"Meaning that you won't tell me?"

She considered him at great length. "You are not," she decided, "a railroad detective. Nor are you a Pinkerton man. I have met many Pinkerton men and they are always very clever and go in for disguises like false beards and such. You are not old enough to grow a beard of any kind, false or otherwise."

Lonnigan flushed. "I'm twenty-two."

"No one would ever guess it. Now I am going to give you some advice which you will not take."

"I know," said Lonnigan. "You are going to tell me to pick up my bedroll and head back for my uncle's horse trap. Dan Goodhue has been singing the same song."

"Which you refuse to heed."

"I refuse to quit," Lonnigan told her with a hint of temper. "I don't like people who lie down before they are dead."

"Dan Goodhue," Tracy told him, "is a man who has already made a compromise with life. He has seen a beautiful woman. He has fallen in love with her, and as

38

long as he can remain in the town where she lives he is willing to become blind to many things."

"Are you by any chance discussing Kate Jacoby?"

"Not by chance," Tracy said grimly. "I am doing it absolutely on purpose. Kate Jacoby is a siren. If she had lived a thousand years ago they would have written books about the way she lured ships to their destruction."

"You don't make much sense," Lonnigan complained.

Tracy's tone became lofty. "I make excellent sense," she told him. "The only trouble is that your knowledge is so limited that you do not comprehend what I am talking about."

"I judge," said Lonnigan, "that you are warning me against Kate Jacoby."

"All the men in the world would be better off if they were warned about her," Tracy said. "But the trouble is that men, being men, and therefore fools, would probably not heed the warning."

Lonnigan grinned. "Well, you're wasting time warning me. Kate Jacoby doesn't know that I'm alive."

"In that," said Tracy, "you have never been more utterly wrong in your life. You, I see, wear pants, and anything that wears pants interests Kate. Such interest is entirely academic with her. She collects men as some people collect old beer bottles."

"You're probably prejudiced," Lonnigan told her. "After all, your father and Jacoby don't seem to get along."

For a moment Tracy McCable was ominously still. Then she said in a different tone, "Mars Jacoby had no business calling my father a thief. Paw is not a thief—he just takes things. He can't help it and he is always sorry afterwards."

Lonnigan stared at her for an instant, thinking she was joking, but the small thin face was very intense and there was no spark in the green eyes.

"Irish people are strange," she said. "You ought to know. You're Irish, although you look more like a Swede. It's Paw's training. In the old country things belonged to the landlord and the landlord was English and any fool knows that it isn't stealing to take something from an Englishman."

Lonnigan chuckled. He had heard Uncle Charley express much the same sentiments.

"And Paw looks on the railroad as a landlord. Besides, he heard that it was partly built with English money." She broke off to nod, then added as if in afterthought, "Of course when I catch him taking things I make him put them back, but I don't always catch him in time and then the money has already been spent at the Big Horn."

"I'm sorry," said Lonnigan, and meant it. "I shouldn't have mentioned it. It's none of my business."

Tracy who had withdrawn a little into her shell relaxed. "Oh, that's all right. Paw isn't the only man in the Junction who drinks, and he doesn't drink often, only when I take my eye off him. I'm not worried about Paw. Paw's old and about everything that can happen to one man has already happened to him. It's you I'm worried about."

"Me?" Lonnigan was startled.

Tracy nodded vehemently. "You. You haven't anyone to take care of you, and anyone knows that a fool man has to be taken care of. And you're young, and you aren't too bright. You are a natural to fall under Kate Jacoby's spell."

"Thanks for the warning."

"Warnings do not do any good," she said sadly. "I have found after much study that no one ever pays attention to warnings. If I thought it would do any good I would warn you that it is Jim Koyner and his outlaws who are attacking the night operators."

"You're certain of that?" Lonnigan was leaning forward across the counter. "You're certain of that, are you?"

She nodded.

"Then why? Koyner isn't a man who does anything merely for the devilment. He must have some plan. What is it?"

Tracy McCable shook her small head. She hated to admit, even to herself, that anything went on around the Junction that she did not know all about, but in this case she was up against a blank wall. She hadn't the slightest idea.

40

TEN

AFTER LEAVING the porch Kate Jacoby climbed the stairs
of the Junction Hotel and, following the long upper hall
to the rear, entered their rooms. The hotel building was
two-storied above the street, but it backed against the
rising canyon wall so that her windows looked out across
the upper ground level.

Her father was still in bed, his heavy body making a
shapeless lump beneath the sheltering blankets. He opened
his eyes at her entrance and blinked. "Why do you always
have to get up before the sun?"

She answered tartly, "It's the most beautiful part of
the day. You used to tell me that when I was a little girl.
You used to take me riding in the early morning."

"I was younger then," he grunted and turned his back
toward her, hoping that she would go on into her own
room and let him sleep.

"Age has nothing to do with it." She was merciless.
"In those days you didn't spend half the night at a poker
table."

Jacoby groaned. These two rooms were his home. The
hotel, as did half the structures in the village, belonged to
him, but he took no part in its active management. This
he left in the capable hands of Mrs. Bishop.

But at times he wished he were back on the ranch, or
at one of the bunkhouses of his various mines—anything
to escape his daughter's constant presence. She annoyed
him and his only defense was to return the annoyance.

He sat up now, his wide shoulders twisting the blankets
as he turned. He kicked the covers free with a vicious
move of his short legs and rested on the edge of the bed,
blinking and yawning widely.

He had slept in his underclothes, which were red, and
which bagged badly at the knees and in the seat. His face
was covered with a stubble of wirelike black beard and
there was the odor of stale whiskey and wet tobacco
about him which made Kate's nose wrinkle in disgust.

Once she had taken a childish pride in the knowledge

that her father was the strongest man in the mountains.
that he could outride, outshoot, and outfight anyone on
his numerous crews. But that day was past. Mars Jacoby
let others do most of his riding now. His girth had in-
creased and he was getting sloppy.

"I'll wait in my room while you dress," she said, and
turned through the connecting door. She heard his grumbled retort and paid no heed. There was a faint slopping
of water from his washstand and a deadened hammering
as he stomped into his boots on the carpeted floor. When
he finally appeared he was fully dressed, even to his
belted gun and wide-brimmed hat, but he had not stopped
to shave.

At their private table in the corner of the narrow dining
room Mrs. Bishop's daughter, Clara, brought their stand-
ard breakfast. She was a girl of seventeen, angular like
her mother, with straw-colored hair and a narrow, sallow,
sullen face.

"How's your mother this morning?" Kate asked the
question from a sense of obligation, not because the state
of Mrs. Bishop's uncertain health really interested her.

"Better." Clara set the platter of eggs on the table and
moved away across the already deserted dining room.

Kate looked after her, frowning. There was something
very disapproving in the girl's manner. Then she looked
at her father.

Mars Jacoby had already attacked his full plate with
the single-mindedness of a bear stoking its belly for a
hard winter. He ate swiftly, thoroughly and with no apparent enjoyment. In contrast, Kate hardly touched her
food, only nibbling at her toast and playing with her egg
until her father had drained his last swallow of coffee.
Then he settled back with a deep sigh and produced a fat
cigar from his pocket.

"I've been wanting to talk to you."

Something in his tone made Kate look up, startled.

"Well, talk." There was no courtesy between them.
There never had been. Mars had always encouraged her
to be blunt-spoken.

"It's Koyner," he said. "Clara told me that he came to
the hotel to see you last night."

"Clara," said Kate, "should pay more attention to her
dishwashing."

Jacoby ignored this. "I've warned you about Koyner
before." His voice was a heavy rumble which he made

42

no effort to lower. Kate was certain that Clara Bishop stood just beyond the kitchen door listening.

"Can't we discuss this at some other time?"

"We'll discuss it now," said Mars Jacoby. "I am a little tired of Mr. Koyner. For a while it amused me to see him taking pot shots at the railroad operators. I'm reaching the point where I find it annoying."

Kate was genuinely alarmed. She well knew that if her father chose to call his hands in from the ranches and go to hunting down Koyner's men in earnest the outlaw's days would be numbered. She tried sarcasm.

"Don't tell me you've suddenly fallen in love with the railroad?"

"I haven't," said Mars Jacoby. "If those damn promoters had stayed in St. Paul and minded their own business this country would have been better off. This country wasn't made for settlers. It's too rough, and the winters are too severe, but that doesn't mean that I've lost my mind, or that I want a trickster like Koyner hanging around my daughter."

"So," she said. "You object to him because he passes a civil word to me rather than because of what he does to the railroad operators."

"And I want him to leave young Lonnigan alone." Jacoby shoved back his chair and rose. "I didn't mind when he ran out the others. They were railroad detectives—Pinkertons. But this boy belongs in the hills. If he gets hurt a lot of mountain people are going to remember his uncle."

He turned then and stalked out, but Kate followed him into the lobby, unwilling to allow him the last word. "What have you got against Jim Koyner?"

Her father stopped and turned, coming back to look up directly into her eyes. "I can understand a horse thief," he said. "A horse thief knows when he throws a saddle on your animal that he is risking his neck. It's the chance he takes—his neck against the value of the horse. But Koyner doesn't play that way. Koyner is like a crooked gambler, fleecing you while he pretends to be your friend. Oh, I know, he's attractive. He has the manners of a gentleman and the morals of an alley cat. Keep away from him."

"And if I don't?"

Mars Jacoby's hand came halfway up as if he would strike her, then he checked himself and said in a curious tone, "I don't understand you, Kate. And yet I should. You are like your mother. I brought her here and gave her everything, and yet she was always unhappy, always disagreeable."

"What did you ever give her?"

He was genuinely startled. "Why, everything that she could want."

Kate's laugh was not a pleasant thing to hear. "Everything . . . You brought her here from Santa Fe. You moved her into a single-room log cabin. You kept her away from people, and life, and happiness . . ."

"Is that what you want?" He was still puzzled.

"That's what I want." She almost spat at him. "I hate these mountains and this miserable town and the played-out mines. I want to go east. I want to go to Europe. I want to have clothes and jewels. I want people to smile at me and recognize me and flatter me. And if Jim Koyner can give me those things, why, I'll go with him."

Mars Jacoby was not used to being defied even by his daughter. For an instant he lost complete control of his temper. His hand lashed out and his spread fingers left marks across the rounded cheek which he slapped.

"Go to your room."

She hesitated.

"I said, go to your room."

She turned then and went quickly up the stairs. He stood and watched her, then with a muttered curse he turned and left the hotel, striding along the sidewalk angrily until he reached the barbershop.

ELEVEN

His BREAKFAST finished, Lonnigan sought the hard bunk in the gabled room of the station, but at noon the westbound sleeper stopped before the lunchroom and the noise of its hungry passengers brought him fully awake. He descended the stairs to find Goodhue busy with freight slips, and after watching the day agent for half an hour he tired of this and crossed the tracks to head up the town's single street.

He was not by choice a town dweller and the Big Horn Saloon held little interest for him. He stopped in Benson's store to buy a box of shells for the Greening and was secretly amused by Larry Benson's reaction. He had the certainty that within the hour the news would be all over town that the new night operator whom everyone had expected to leave was buying buckshot.

The knowledge brought back to him the problem of the attacks on the station and his brow furrowed thoughtfully. Outside the store he met Mars Jacoby on the sidewalk, and Jacoby, paused, removing his ever-present cigar from his lips.

"How do you like working for the railroad by now?"

Lonnigan looked for irony in the question and found none. "All right," he stammered.

"No trouble?" said Jacoby.

"None to speak of," the boy told him.

Jacoby nodded and moved on. Lonnigan looked after him thoughtfully, then crossed and walked into the livery stable. Why was it, he thought, that whenever anyone asked him a direct question he stammered, and then a curious puzzle presented itself. Through his whole conversation that morning with Tracy McCable he could not recall stammering once.

He thought about this all the time the livery man was saddling a rented horse. He could not recall ever having talked with a stranger without his usual speech difficulty. Uncle Charley and the three riders at the home ranch had been different. He had seldom stammered with them.

45

The man brought the horse and he was about to mount when Kate Jacoby came in through the arch of the door. Sight of her stopped him, holding him speechless.

Kate was as startled as he was. She had spent the full morning in her hotel room, too furious at her father to stir outside. But by noon she had had enough of her own company and as usual, when she wanted a chance to think, she had decided to ride up the canyon.

Her smile was instinctive. It was beyond Kate's power to keep from flirting mildly with any man, and she nodded as she moved past him, saying, "So you're leaving the Junction so soon."

"Only for a ride." He managed to get the words out without mangling them. "It's a beautiful day for a ride, Miss Kate."

Here was an invitation which she was about to refuse, then another thought came and she stopped, turning. "That's what I thought. If you'll wait until Alf saddles my horse I'll ride with you."

Never in his wildest dreams had Randell Lonnigan considered the possibility of riding with Kate Jacoby. In itself the name Jacoby would have made him or any other rider hesitate. She was old Mars's only child, and in Lonnigan's opinion Mars Jacoby was probably one of the wealthiest men in the world, nearly as wealthy in fact as the mysterious group who owned the railroad and ran it from far-off St. Paul and Chicago. He did not realize that most of Jacoby's mines were worked out, or that the blizzards for three years running had wiped out a good two thirds of the Jacoby cattle. A man is as rich as his reputation, and Jacoby had been reputed a wealthy man for years.

He waited until her horse was saddled and held the stirrup for her, and together they rode up the street toward the canyon mouth.

Their passage did not go unobserved. Mars Jacoby watched them from the door of the Big Horn. Clara Bishop paused in her washing of one of the front hotel windows, and Jocko Halleran, coming from Todd's blacksmith shop, paused and stepped back out of sight as they went past, his heavy, cruel face lighting with something which might have been called a smile.

The canyon lifted steeply above the town, a deep gorge which the quick-running river had ripped through the stone barrier of the hills.

The trail was narrow, and the timber with its long evergreen needles grew thickly, seeming to sprout from the very rocks themselves. The air was thin, and cold, but they were both mountain-bred and acclimated to its thin oxygen content. The trail looped back and forth, sometimes running on the very brink of the brawling stream, at others curving away until the racing water was little more than a murmur behind the masking timber.

As they rode, stirrup to stirrup, the girl from time to time glanced sidewise at Lonnigan. He was, she saw, taller than she remembered, and there was a solidness about him which told of strength despite his deceptively slender appearance.

Lonnigan was not unconscious of her glances and he found that he was unusually tongue-tied, that no matter how he tried he could think of absolutely nothing to say.

For her part Kate was thinking of him not as a man, but as a danger to their plans. As long as he remained at the station Jim Koyner would not rest easy, and yet she could not forget her father's warning of that morning. If there were another attack on Lonnigan, Jacoby would certainly act.

Why, she wondered, had fate decreed that Lonnigan come to the Junction on this particular week? If his arrival had been a week later the Silk Express would have already made its run, the holdup be an accomplished fact and Koyner and his men would have vanished from the mountains.

It therefore became necessary for her to do one of two things—persuade Lonnigan that he should leave voluntarily, or keep Koyner from acting until the night of the holdup itself. The first course would be the simplest and she set herself to use the weapon which she understood best and which she had found effective with almost any man she had ever met.

The trail looped around an upthrust which jutted from the canyon wall, and a small grassed meadow opened to the right, running back to the stream beyond.

She turned her horse aside and saw Lonnigan follow, and halted her animal with a gentle pressure of the rein. "I think my saddle girth is loose," she said. "It's slipping a little and the trail gets steeper above." She started to dismount, but Lonnigan was before.

He stepped from his saddle and offered her his hand. Kate, who could ride as well as any man and better than

47

most, was awkward in her descent. She reached the ground, took half a step. Apparently her heel caught and she started to fall forward.

Automatically Lonnigan's arms went out to catch her, and she slumped forward against his chest. For an instant he stood holding her, not knowing quite what to do, then he bent his head.

"Are you . . . you all . . . right?"

She straightened and one of her arms slipped around his neck and the next instant she kissed the surprised Lonnigan directly on the lips. He was rigid with surprise, then instinct took charge and he returned the kiss with enthusiasm.

To Kate's amazement she found herself a prisoner in a pair of arms that felt as unbreakable as steel bands. "Well . . ." She managed to push herself back a little. "Well."

Lonnigan was immediately filled with contriteness. "I . . . I . . . I don't know what happened to me."

Kate knew very well what had happened to him. She had seen much more experienced men than Lonnigan weaken before her kisses, and she smiled a little to herself as she stepped clear, managing to appear a perfect picture of confusion.

"You seem to have had a great deal of practice, Ran Lonnigan."

Lonnigan was flattered. Almost any male is flattered when told by a beautiful woman that he is adroit at love-making, although the truth is that few men are the equal of an unexperienced woman.

"Honest . . ." said Lonnigan. "I . . . I haven't hardly kissed any girls . . . much."

Kate was straightening her jacket. "It's all right," she said. "I've wondered what you were like ever since that dance at Falling Leaf two years ago. But probably you don't remember."

Lonnigan remembered very well. Dancing with Kate that night had been one of the high points in his life, but he had had no idea that she would recall it. She had danced with almost everyone in the big room that evening.

"Gee," he said. "You remembered . . . you . . ."

He didn't finish the sentence, for a noise behind him made him turn instinctively. A rider had come off the trail and was sitting loosely in his saddle staring at them.

48

The man's clothes were worn and nondescript, but his face was what drew and held Lonnigan's attention. The whole left side was puckered and red and angry-looking, as if it had been seared with a hot iron or scalded with live steam. Afterwards Lonnigan thought he would have recognized the rider for who he was, even if Kate hadn't drawn a sharp breath, saying quickly without thinking:

"Chad Crawford! What are you doing here?"

Crawford. Lonnigan's mind snapped back to Bullock's words about the dead telegraph operator, and he realized that he was facing the mysterious ghost and that Crawford seemed very much alive. At least he had pulled his gun and it was pointing unwaveringly at Lonnigan's stomach.

TWELVE

IT WAS NOT in Ran Lonnigan to be afraid. Uncle Charley had seen to that. Uncle Charley had told him when he was first large enough to pack a gun: "A gun's for use, like a saddle or bridle. It isn't to play with, but a lot of people wear guns who shouldn't be turned loose with a sharpened stick. If you're going to wear that you'd better know how to use it."

Lonnigan had learned how to use it, with the same patience which he exhibited in mastering the telegraph key, and he felt perfectly confident of his own ability.

But looking up at the mounted man, at Chad Crawford's scarred face and at the deep anger in the black eyes, he realized that he had no chance to draw his gun. He stood there, his hands carefully away from his hips, watching Crawford without change of expression.

It was Kate Jacoby who moved. She thrust her body between the two men, her black eyes blazing. "Chad, have you lost your mind? Put that gun away."

Crawford hesitated. Few people could face Kate Jacoby down and he was not one of these. There was a streak of irresponsibility about the man, a lack of schooled discipline, which showed now as he backed his horse so that he would have a clear shot at Lonnigan.

But the girl, reading his purpose, shifted with him. "You heard what I said. Do you want to fight with me?"

Crawford let his gun sag. It was very evident that he did not want to fight with Kate Jacoby. "But I saw you . . ."

"Never mind what you saw," she told him. "Just put that gun away and ride out. I'll talk with you later."

"But Kate . . ." His tone was loaded with unhappy appeal.

"Do as I tell you if you ever want me to speak to you again."

He holstered the gun then and swung the horse, driving the long roweled spurs against its flanks so that it all but leaped from under him. Neither Lonnigan nor the girl

50

moved until Crawford reached the trail, turned into it and spurred up along the rising ground until he rounded the next bend and was lost to sight.

Kate Jacoby let out her held breath slowly; then she turned and the smile she gave Lonnigan was warmly possessive. Lonnigan was staring after Crawford. He felt as if he had really seen a ghost. There was no doubt about it—the scar-faced man had intended to kill him, and but for Kate Jacoby's presence would have done so.

"Whooo!"

She said, trying to speak lightly, "Don't mind Chad."

"I don't mind him," said Lonnigan slowly, "but I'd hate to meet him unless you were along."

"Chad," she said, "isn't quite right in the head." Her brain had worked swiftly and she had already decided on the story which she would tell Lonnigan. She had to tell him the truth in part, since it was obvious by his manner that he knew who Crawford was. "He used to be a station operator for the railroad."

Lonnigan nodded. "They think he's dead."

"He might well be—poor Chad." She made her tone very sad. "He did a brave thing, jumping into that train wreck. But it's affected his mind."

Lonnigan looked at her. "But why doesn't the railroad know?"

"The railroad," she almost spat the word. Then she said contritely, "But I forget, you're working for the railroad."

"That doesn't matter." Lonnigan hadn't intended to say that. He found that when he was with Kate Jacoby he was never entirely certain what he would say.

"The railroad is cold-blooded," Kate told him. "We knew that and we all knew what Chad had done. So we took care of him. He's living up in the hills at one of Father's ranches. Sometimes he dosen't even know who he is."

"But what made him go gunning for me?"

She widened her eyes and a flush crept up to color her full cheeks. "He must have seen you kissing me. He . . . he thinks he's in love with me."

"In love with you?"

She was a beautiful picture of confusion. "I helped the doctor take care of him," she explained. "It was natural, the doctor said, for him to fall in love with me."

"I . . . I can understand that," Lonnigan stammered a little. His throat felt a little dry.

51

"Can you?" She gave him an arch look. "The doctor said that he shouldn't be worried, that I was to encourage him."

"You're sweet," said Lonnigan, and meant it.

"No, I'm not," she denied. "But I feel so sorry for the poor boy. That's why we didn't tell the railroad. The doctor said there would be an investigation and reports, and that would worry Chad and make him lose the little mind he has left. You won't tell them, will you—I mean about him being alive?"

"I . . ."

"Of course you are working for the railroad. I know that, but sometimes it's more important to think of a poor man than it is of the railroad."

"Well . . ." Lonnigan was struggling to think clearly. "Tell me one thing. Bullock said that he saw Chad Crawford buried. If Crawford is alive, who did they bury?"

"Oh," she said, "a poor tramp. He was hiding behind the tender and he beat Crawford to the engine. He was so badly burned that they couldn't tell who he was, but some of the crew had seen Crawford running down the track and assumed it was him."

"And one thing more," Lonnigan was persistent. "These attacks on the station at night?"

Kate was thinking fast. Her story had grown as she talked and she saw a nice way out.

"Oh, those," she said. "Some of the cowboys from Dad's ranch ride down with Chad at night. He likes to send messages over the telegraph, so they run the night operators out of his way."

Lonnigan stared at her. The explanation sounded fantastic, but it was also so simple. And he knew cowboys. If Jacoby's riders took it into their heads that Crawford ought to break into the station they would not hesitate to run the night operators out of the way. They were, most of them, overdeveloped adolescents who loved practical jokes. The fact that their actions might bother the railroad would not trouble them in the least.

"You know," he said, "I'd like to tell Mr. Bullock. I only met him once, but I think he would see the joke."

"Please don't." Kate Jacoby reached out and grasped both his hands. If Lonnigan insisted on telling Bullock, all her lies would be useless. All Kate was doing was trying to gain time. "Wait a few days," she pleaded. "The

52

doctor is going to examine Chad against next week. If he says it's all right then you can tell Bullock."

"All right," Lonnigan agreed reluctantly.

"You're sweet," Kate said and, putting her hands on his shoulders, stood on tiptoe to press her warm mouth against his. "You are very sweet, but I must get back." She stepped away from him, glancing at the watch she wore pinned to her waist. "Heavens. I had no idea it was so late."

Lonnigan moved back to her horse and tested the saddle girth. Kate smiled. "You know," she said, "I don't believe it's loose after all."

Lonnigan turned to look at her, and suddenly they were both laughing like a couple of children.

After he had helped her to mount and they'd turned back down the trail, riding close together, he said, "You know . . . you aren't at all like I thought."

"What did you think?" She glanced at him sideways.

"Well . . ." he fumbled, again having difficulty with words. "I used to see you at dances, and you were Mars Jacoby's daughter and every rider in the country was in love with you and I didn't figure I had a chance."

She turned to look directly at the trail ahead, asking in a low voice. "Did you want a chance?"

"I . . . sure . . . What man wouldn't?"

"I am Mars Jacoby's daughter," she told him, "but I'm also myself. I . . . I have feelings like anyone else."

He rode in close and would have reached out to put an arm around her, but she stopped him. "Not now. We might meet someone else on the trail."

Lonnigan was a little sulky. "I'll begin to believe that Sis was right."

"Sis?"

"The McCable girl. She warned me that you were a dangerous woman."

For an instant Kate's smile was frozen on her lips, then she managed to say in a light voice, "So you've been discussing me with the McCable child. I don't think I like that."

"Ah . . ." Lonnigan was embarrassed again. "She didn't mean a thing. She was just sore because Mars called her father a thief."

"He is a thief," said Kate Jacoby, "and a drunkard, to boot. I think if I were Tracy McCable I would be very careful how I talked about anyone."

53

THIRTEEN

It was nearing dark when Chad Crawford rode into Jim Koyner's camp, set high in the mountain meadow above the new dam sight. This was not Koyner's permanent headquarters which was to the eastward in the Hole-in-the-Wall. There were a dozen cabins there, a kind of town to which the outlaws retreated when for any reason the surrounding country became too warm for them.

This camp was temporary, only a few hours' ride from the Junction. From here Koyner and his men made their plans and waited the word that the Silk Express had left Seattle and was speeding eastward.

Koyner sat with his back to a lean-to built against a rock shelf. He was warming his hands at the small fire, for the day was cold, nor did he rise as Crawford rode up. He watched as the scar-faced man dismounted and moved toward the fire, ignoring the other men who were sprawled around on the hard ground.

Koyner frowned as he noted Crawford's face. "What's the matter with you?"

Crawford hunkered down at Koyner's side. He was a big man and he looked bulkier than usual in his heavy fleece-lined brush jacket.

"I saw Kate on the trail." He spoke in an undertone so that his voice would not carry to Indian Pete who lay on a dirty saddle blanket half a dozen feet away. "She was with the new night station agent. She was kissing him."

Koyner found the news surprising, but no sign of emotion marred his handsome face. "So? I suppose she can kiss him if she wants to."

Crawford said angrily, "She shouldn't. It ain't decent. She is going to marry me."

Koyner made no comment. He had very little use for the scar-faced man, considering him rather stupid. Nor had he been too pleased with Kate's idea that she could bring Crawford into their camp by making the man love her. It wasn't that Koyner was jealous. He held himself

54

above jealousy and he certainly did not have any fear that Crawford would win Kate away from him.

It was only that it was a nuisance keeping the real state of affairs away from the ex-station agent. Crawford was useful. On more than one night he had crouched outside some way station listening to the messages which flowed across the telegraph line; he had broken into the deserted station at the Junction, sitting on the key and picking up the gossip which the operators relayed to one another during the slack periods. The one trouble was that Crawford could not resist the impulse to occasionally send garbled messages himself, which messages had led to the stories that had traveled up and down the line of the ghost at the Junction.

But Crawford's main usefulness would come on the night of the holdup. Then he would take over the Junction key, making certain that the railroad made no move which would interfere with their plans. On that night the Junction station must be empty, which meant getting rid of this Lonnigan.

But Koyner said nothing of this to Crawford. Instead he told him angrily, "I told you when you first agreed to come in with us that you should not ride the trails or go into town during daylight. We don't want the railroad to know that you are alive. Did this Lonnigan recognize you?"

One of Crawford's hands rose to his scarred cheek and his fingers moved along the reddened lumpish face. "I guess so."

Koyner rose. He came up in one single, swift motion. "Pete." The half-breed was instantly upright. "Get Jocko and three horses. We're riding in. The rest of you stay here—and I mean here." His eyes swept the silent circle, then he looked at Crawford, saying without emphasis, "That goes for you too. If you aren't here when I get back I'll have Pete track you down and kill you."

The Indian's smile was wolfish. Chad Crawford shuddered. Unstable as he was, he held a healthy respect for both Koyner and the breed. But he could not resist saying, "If you see her, tell her I'm sorry. I didn't mean to start anything, but seeing her let him kiss her . . ."

Koyner took a step forward and caught Crawford by the lapels of his heavy coat. Crawford outweighed Koyner by a good thirty pounds, but such was the outlaw's strength that he lifted the other man clear of the ground,

55

holding him thus for a full minute before he set him back on his feet.

"Listen to me." Koyner's voice was even and unhurried and deadly. "I care nothing for your personal quarrels. Those are your business, but if you jeopardize what I've been planning for six months, I won't bother to call Pete. I'll handle you myself." He turned then and walked toward the horse which the Indian was already saddling.

The lights in the windows along the Junction's street were fully bright by the time Koyner and his men burst out of the canyon, hammered across the small bridge and pulled in at the rack before the hotel.

Dan Goodhue was just leaving the lobby and heading for his nightly game at the Big Horn as Koyner stepped to the ground, flung the reins to Jocko Halleran and came storming up the steps. The outlaw did not so much as glance in Goodhue's direction, but pushed by him and into the lobby.

Goodhue hesitated, then, realizing that both Halleran and Indian Pete were watching him from their horses, he came on across the porch, descended the steps and moved down the street. But instead of continuing toward the Big Horn Saloon as was his custom, he waited until he thought he was not observed and then ducked between the livery stable and the barbershop.

The buildings were built in shelflike holes which had been cut out of the canyon sides, and he skirted them one after another until he reached the door of the hotel kitchen. He peered in, finding the room empty, for Clara had already gone upstairs to tend her sick mother, and entered.

By nature Dan Goodhue was not a sneaking person, but the impulse to spy on Kate and Jim Koyner was more than he could resist. The dining room beyond the kitchen was in darkness and he slipped into it, moving silently between the ghostly tables until he was close to the lobby door. He was in time to hear Kate's voice from the lobby.

"But still, you shouldn't have come." She sounded annoyed. "I had a fight with Dad this morning. He told me not to see you again."

Koyner's laugh was musical. "That," he said, "is like telling water not to run downhill. Come here and kiss me."

"Jim, listen." She was still protesting. "We're so close—

56

so very close—to everything we've planned. What if someone saw us? We have to be careful. We can't afford for Dad to line up against you. What if Crad Crawford rode in? I met the fool on the trail today."

Goodhue's hands were knotted at his sides, his thin face drawn tightly across the jawbones with the force of his suffering. He wanted to get out of there, to hear no more, but he found that it was impossible to move.

"I know," he heard Koyner say. "That's why I'm here. Crawford came into camp this evening. He was nearly wild. He'd caught you kissing the new station man."

There was a long silence from the lobby, then Kate's voice, with a hint of defensive mockery, "Don't tell me you are jealous?"

"Not me," Jim Koyner told her. "Only a fool is jealous. It's a sign that a person feels inferior and I never feel inferior, darling. If a woman seems to favor a lesser man I merely put her down as a fool and forget her."

Kate laughed. "Sometimes I should hate you."

"Do that," he told her. "It might be interesting. But, this Lonnigan . . . ?"

"He's a green boy," she said, "and easy."

"And hardly worth your time?"

Her tone got startled. "You don't think I kissed him for amusement? He's trouble, Jim. For some reason Dad has decided that he should be protected. If you run Lonnigan away from the station there will be the devil to pay."

"Are you telling me this because you have some interest in him?"

"You aren't nearly as smart as you lead yourself to believe," she said. "I'm making Lonnigan my friend. I asked him this afternoon not to tell Bullock that he had seen Crawford, and he promised. I'll keep him in line until our time comes. Then on the right night you can run him out."

Koyner was thinking aloud. "You may have something there. I don't want to call the Division Point's attention to the Junction this week. If you can hold him in line . . ."

"Since when have I ever failed to hold a man in line?"

He chuckled. "You know, Kate, you have all the instincts of a tramp. Women like you have built up power for themselves through the ages by controlling men."

She said, "And how else can a woman operate? It's a

57

man's world, Jim. A woman can use the only tools that have been given her . . ."

Dan Goodhue felt as if he were being stifled. Blindly he turned and stumbled toward the kitchen door, bumping against a table in the process. But if the two in the lobby heard they took no action, for he reached the outer door without interruption and forged out into the clear chill darkness.

He stopped, filling his lungs with the sharp air, and stared upward through the notch between the wall of the building and the cut-out bank at the sky far above.

I should kill him, he thought. I should kill her. I should kill both of them. They are up to something, and I could stop it. But he knew that he would not, that he would take no action of any kind. He moved across the rough ground and came back to the street at the point from which he had left.

He turned then and crossed to the Big Horn, pushing through the bat-wing doors and pausing at the bar. Long before midnight he was drunk, and when he drank he no longer seemed to care.

FOURTEEN

UNCONSCIOUS of the effect that his presence had on a number of people at the Junction, Ran Lonnigan sat at the table in the bay listening to the traffic as it flowed up and down the wire.

The central window had been repaired and he felt something like a tin duck sitting unhappily in a shooting gallery. Certainly he offered a conspicuous target for any marksman lurking in the darkness beyond the tracks. His impulse had been to put out the big swinging center lamp, but he forced himself not to touch it. After all, he reasoned, the railroad had not sent him to the Junction to crouch in the darkness.

But the shotgun, loaded and ready, rested against his leg beneath the table, and his plans were fully made. At the first sign of trouble he meant to drop below the table, seize the gun, knock out the lamp and then wait for the intruders.

His ear was primed for any foreign sound above the chatter of the key, and twice he had moved convulsively when some night animal had scurried along the platform.

So when sound finally reached him, instead of jumping as he had planned, he listened, trying to locate its source, then straightened and quickly blew out the lamp. A moment later, with the shotgun held across his body, he slipped from the rear door to the back platform and edged his way across the walkway which led to the lunchroom.

Two figures were coming toward him across the foot of the main street. He caught their silhouettes in the store lamps and, waiting in deep shadow, watched as they reached the tracks and started across. Then with a rush of relief he realized that it was Tracy and her father and moved forward.

The old man seemed to be having difficulty with his feet and he was arguing heatedly with the girl. "I'm all right. Just let me alone." He broke from her grasp, mounted the ballast of the right-of-way and attempted to step over the tracks. But his boot heel caught on the rail and he sprawled headlong.

Tracy gave a little cry, running toward him, and Lonnigan came from the shadows quickly and bent to catch the old man's arm. Not until then had Tracy been conscious of his presence.

Between them they helped her father to his feet, and the girl said quickly, "You all right?"

"Perfectly. Absolutely all right." The words were so blurred and his brogue so heavy that they were almost indistinguishable, but they relieved the girl and she turned her attention to Lonnigan. He had stepped aside, expecting to be thanked, but he was wrong.

"What do you mean, spying on us?" Tracy McCable sounded really angry.

"I wasn't spying."

"What do you call it, standing in the shadows and watching decent people when they're . . . when they're sick?"

Lonnigan's own temper rose to meet hers. "I wasn't spying. You don't think I'd carry this gun just to watch a drunken . . ."

"Don't say it," said Tracy McCable. "Don't you dare say it. We've got enough enemies in this town who are just waiting to run back to Bullock and tell him that Terry has slipped and taken one too many . . ." Her voice broke a little. "I suppose that's what you'll do—go right into the station and wire Dawson."

Lonnigan's mouth opened, then closed slowly. She was the second woman to ask him not to tell the railroad something, and the approach that the two girls used was so utterly different that it was startling.

He said stiffly, "I'm no talebearer. And if your father wants to drink that's his business."

"He doesn't want to," said Tracy. "He just can't help it. He's . . . he's weak."

"That's right," Terry McCable agreed amiably. "That's it. I'm just weak." He swayed and would have toppled forward had not Lonnigan caught him.

"Here," Lonnigan handed the gun to the girl. "Hold this." He stooped then and caught up Terry McCable as if he had been a baby and turned toward the station.

"Where are you going?"

"Why . . ." He stopped. "I was going to put him up in my bunk."

"There's a couch in the storeroom." She fumbled with some keys, found the right one and opened the lunchroom door. "Wait until I light the lamp."

He waited, hearing her move about inside, then a friction match flared as the wick in the lamp caught. "In here."

Terry McCable had gone to sleep. He lay in Lonnigan's arms as relaxed as a child and as untroubled. Lonnigan carried him around the counter and through the swinging door into the kitchen. The girl had lighted a second lamp and was unlocking the storeroom door.

Inside, flanked by the boxed goods, was a narrow cot on which Lonnigan laid the sleeping man. He wondered as he did so just how many times Terry McCable had occupied the same couch and for the same reason. Then he followed Tracy out and watched her close the door.

For an instant she leaned against the wall, pressing the back of her hand against her mouth in a little gesture of tired hopelessness, then her natural vitality came to the rescue and she straightened, saying almost shyly, "I'm sorry for the nasty things I said outside."

"Ah," said Lonnigan, "that's all right. Uncle Charley used to have a bottle now and then. A doctor told him it was good medicine."

"It isn't a bottle now and then," she said, and there was no pretense about her. "It's whenever he can get one. Bullock warned him that if he was caught again he was through. And if he was fired here he'd be finished for good."

Lonnigan did not know quite what to say.

"It's because he's disappointed," said Tracy. "All his life he has dreamed of being important, but somehow he never was. He thought in the old country, if he could only come to America—away from the English—everything would be fine. But when he got here it wasn't any different."

Lonnigan still didn't know what to say, and Tracy noticed his embarrassment. "I'll get some coffee." Her manner changed. "I shouldn't be telling you my troubles. You've got troubles of your own." She moved over to the stove and put on the coffeepot.

While they waited for it to boil she boosted herself onto the table and sat swinging her heels. "Terry's all right," she said, "as long as I can keep money from him and keep an eye on him. But when he gets a thirst he

61

will do anything for a drink, and when he has had a drink he loses all his perspective."

"Maybe," said Lonnigan, "you could say something to the bartenders—about selling it to him, I mean."

Tracy's green eyes flashed. "I wouldn't be doing a thing like that, ever," she told him tartly. "A man has his pride which you must not hurt, and you don't tell everyone your business. This is my problem and I'll thank you not to mention it along the street."

"I had no intention of mentioning it," Lonnigan assured her.

Tracy rose, got the coffeepot and two thick cups. When hers was sweetened to suit her she said, "I see you didn't take my advice."

He looked at her in surprise. "What are you talking about now?"

"I saw you riding in with Kate Jacoby just before dark."

"Oh, that," he laughed in relief, welcoming the chance to talk about Kate. "You've got her all wrong," he said. "She's the kindest-hearted person that I ever met."

"Is she, now?" Tracy's tone was deceptively mild.

"She is," said Lonnigan warmly. "It's just that you don't understand her."

"A mouse always thinks it understands a trap until it is caught."

Lonnigan's laugh was genuine. "Meaning that I'm a mouse and that Kate is trying to catch me?"

"You understand rapidly," Tracy told him dryly. "I only have to hit you on the head a little."

"But why should Kate Jacoby want to trap me?"

"That," said Tracy, "is something that I am giving my full consideration. You are not, by certain standards, too bad-looking."

Lonnigan's chuckle was a little rueful. "You aren't very free with your compliments," he said.

"There are two schools of thought," she told him. "One says that the way to win a man is to flatter him, the other is to keep him guessing."

Lonnigan's smile faded a little and he said in half-seriousness, "Are you trying to say that you are interested in me yourself?"

"That is another thing which I have not quite decided."

"A girl," he told her, "should never be forward. A girl

62

is supposed to sit quietly and wait until a man notices her of his own free will."

"That," said Tracy, "is utter stuff and nonsense. I'll bet you read it in a book."

"I didn't," Lonnigan flushed a little, not knowing quite how to take this. "Uncle Charley told me and . . ."

"Was Uncle Charley married?" Tracy asked.

Lonnigan shook his head.

"Then I would decide that Uncle Charley was not much of an authority. Did Kate wait for you to kiss her this afternoon, or did she manage to stumble and fall into your arms?"

Lonnigan was caught off guard. "Why how did . . . ?"

"The technique is not new," Tracy told him. "And Kate has never been what you might call an original person. She merely takes the work of others and perfects it for her own uses."

Lonnigan was stung to retort: "That shows that you don't know her. You don't know for instance that the station agent who was scalded in that train wreck is not dead, that Kate helped the doctor nurse him back to health, but that the poor fellow is not entirely right in the head."

"You're referring to Chad Crawford, I suppose?"

Lonnigan stared at her. "Do you mean to tell me that you knew that Crawford was still alive?"

"Almost everyone in the Junction knows it."

"Then why didn't some of them tell the railroad?"

"Because," said Tracy, "Chad Crawford preferred to remain dead as far as the record goes, and, as you should know, in this country people do not concern themselves with the business of others. Also, it has tickled the people to hear the ghost stories which are whispered up and down the right of way. It is a joke, and there is little enough to laugh at in these hills."

"But you mean . . ."

"I mean that anything that is the matter with Chad Crawford's head was put there by Kate."

"I don't believe you. I've seen him. I know he is not quite sane."

"Few men are," Tracy said sadly, "After Kate gets hold of them. She's worse than an epidemic. In fact she is a whole series of epidemics all rolled up into one."

FIFTEEN

LONNIGAN spent the rest of the night listening to the messages which flowed up and down the line. Twice he reached for the key, prepared to flash the news to Dawson that there was no ghost, that Chad Crawford was alive. But both times he changed his mind, remembering his promise to Kate.

He found that he simply could not believe the things Tracy had said. He felt of course that Tracy was honest, but he also felt that she was suffering from a cross between jealousy of the older girl and a dislike of the Jacoby family in general.

"A funny little kid." He muttered the words aloud. "She's got trouble with that father of hers, but she doesn't whine. She takes it with her chin up."

A lumber freight whistled from the west and Lonnigan rose, pulling on his brush jacket, and stepped out onto the platform to see it sweep past.

The fireman waved, and he raised his hand in return, wishing that he was on the train, that he too was sweeping eastward.

After the caboose lights had vanished into the canyon, he still stood before the station looking across the tracks and up the rutted width of the Junction's single street. The town slept. There was a faint light from the hotel lobby where an all-night lamp was always kept burning, and before the Big Horn two horses stood shot-legged and patient, waiting for their owners, who lingered within. The rest of the town was in full darkness.

Lonnigan filled his lungs, using the sharp cold air to fight off a dragging desire toward sleep. The sky was nearly clear, with only a few puffs of clouds hanging above the western peaks and blending with the dark mountains until it was impossible to tell where the rugged ground ended and the vapor masses began. The stars were bright, winking down through the thinnish air, and a rind of moon was far down in the sky, telling Lonnigan how late it was. He turned and went back into the station.

As the waves of stale heat struck him, he shivered a little and stood hunched in his heavy coat a moment to let the cold seep from his hands and face.

In the morning he put the problem of Chad Crawford up to Dan Goodhue. The day man arrived a little before his accustomed time, for he had not lingered on the porch to see Kate Jacoby appear.

I'd speak to her, Goodhue thought. If I saw her this morning I'd tell her that I was listening last night while she talked with Koyner.

He had hurried through his breakfast and then headed down the street directly for the station, noting as he crossed the tracks that the new bay window which had been installed the preceding day was still in place.

Koyner, he thought, has listened to Kate and has not had the new night operator attacked. He wondered again what Koyner was up to, and then put it from his mind, as he pushed open the door and came into the waiting room.

Lonnigan was glad to see him. He had spent the last hour pacing up and down the office, dissatisfied and uncertain.

He said, almost at once, "I had a strange experience yesterday. I met a man who is supposed to be dead."

"Well?" said Dan Goodhue, removing his hat and replacing it with his green eyeshade.

"He's the ghost," said Lonnigan. "You must have known him when he was alive. I mean . . ." he stammered a little, "before they buried him."

Goodhue was not surprised.

"And he's very much alive." Lonnigan was still stumbling a little over his words. "I was with Kate Jacoby and she made me promise that I wouldn't tell Bullock or anyone else at the Division Point."

For an instant Goodhue felt the stabbing thrust of jealousy. Never in the whole time that he had been at the Junction had Kate Jacoby ever gone riding with him. Then he put the thought away from him, for he knew deep in his heart that the girl had no more use for Lonnigan than she had for a dozen other men. It was not Lonnigan who was his rival, or even Chad Crawford. It was Koyner.

He said slowly, "If you promised . . . ?"

"I promised," said Lonnigan, and was miserable.

"Then I don't see how . . ."

"Look." Lonnigan was spacing his words, taking time to form each one properly. "I'm working for the railroad, and I think they ought to know."

"Why?" said Goodhue. "What possible help would it be if Bullock knew that Crawford is alive?"

"Then you already knew?"

"Of course."

Lonnigan had the impulse to ask him if the story that Kate had told about Crawford being unbalanced from the accident was true. But somehow he did not want to discuss it further with the small sandy man. Goodhue had been an employee of the Pacific Northern much longer than he had, and Goodhue had known that Crawford was alive. If Goodhue did not think it important to relay the information to Bullock, Lonnigan felt that he would probably be making a fool of himself by doing so.

He turned away then and, picking up his jacket, went toward the lunchroom and breakfast.

SIXTEEN

JOCKO HALLERAN was a man who loved cards. He would pull a greasy deck from his pocket and play on a saddle blanket or on the floor of a cave. Whenever his operations with Jim Koyner brought him close enough to the Junction, he spent most of his time at the poker table at the rear of the Big Horn.

He was there now, in fact he had been there since eleven o'clock that morning, bent intently above the table edge, his big broken hands grasping the cards tightly, his small fugitive eyes watching each player in turn from beneath the shelter of his bushy brows.

Jocko was not old, but he had started as a laborer at sixteen and he was prematurely marked. He had killed his first man with a pick handle in a Texas railroad camp because he thought the man cheated at cards. After that he had lost count, but when he thought about it—which was seldom—he reckoned that through the years he must have accounted for at least a dozen, not counting Mexicans and Indians.

He had for the most part been a lone wolf, since he was not a sociable man, but a chance meeting with Jim Koyner had changed his life. Koyner had captured Jocko's imagination. His stories of confidence swindles, of bilking the rich and the secure, had fired Jocko's enthusiasm, and he had joined Koyner's band, being as nearly a lieutenant as the outlaw leader would tolerate.

He did not see Ran Lonnigan enter the saloon, and was not conscious of the new night operator's presence until he sensed that someone was looking at the cards across his shoulder and turned to see who it was.

Jocko believed firmly that if anyone else saw the cards he was holding it would bring bad luck, and his temper which was always on edge came up to blind him. He threw the hand in the middle of the table and came out of his chair with the quickness of a cat.

"You," he said. "Don't you know enough to keep your damn nose to yourself?"

67

Ran Lonnigan was too startled to answer for a moment. He had slept until almost two-thirty, eaten lunch at the lunchroom, half hoping for a sight of Tracy. But the redheaded girl was absent and Terry McCable, made taciturn by his night of drinking, had waited on him in sullen silence.

McCable had no memory of the preceding evening. He did not realize that Lonnigan had helped to bed him down in the storeroom, and if he had, it would have made no difference.

After the lunch, feeling restless and in need of companionship, Lonnigan had returned to the station. But Goodhue was also in no mood for talk, and after half a dozen unsuccessful attempts to draw him out, Lonnigan had given up and crossed the tracks to move slowly along the Junction's main street.

He paused in the barbershop for a shave, but the Italian barber's accent was so pronounced that he could barely understand what the man said.

It was in this mood that he entered the Big Horn and, ignoring the long bar, moved back to watch the poker game. There were only four players, and the big room held less than a dozen men. Lonnigan had taken his stand behind Jocko's chair, not because he knew the man, but because he sat facing Mars Jacoby, and Lonnigan wanted to study Kate's father when he thought that he was not observed.

Jocko's sudden attack caught him off balance, but his humor, being uncertain at his waking, had not been improved by McCable's rudeness, Goodhue's attitude or the jabbering of the Italian barber.

He reached out, hardly thinking what he did, and caught the front of Jocko's stained shirt, pulling the heavier man to him with his left hand, while he drove the right fist against the stubble which covered Halleran's long jaw.

Jocko went down, crashing backward against the chair so that it collapsed with his weight. The broken chair probably saved Lonnigan's life, for even as he fell Jocko was clawing at the big gun which he wore tied down against his hip.

It was as senseless as most barroom fights are—without real meaning or real feeling on either side. But the broken chair hampered Halleran's movements, and before he could get the gun free and raise it Lonnigan stepped in and kicked his wrist sharply.

The gun flew clear across the room, crashing barrel-first downward into a battered brass cuspidor which stood against the wall.

Jocko let out a yell, dropping back against the dirty floor, nursing his wrist, and Lonnigan thought that the fight was finished.

But Indian Pete was leaning against the short end of the bar where it made a curve to join the wall below the poker table. He straightened now, his hand going to the knife in his belt, and he moved forward, careful and alert and deadly.

Jim Koyner sat on the other side of the room, his chair tilted back against the wall, his boot heels hooked over the lower rung, his hat pulled down so that it was hardly possible to see his face. Lonnigan had not even noticed him when he came in, but Koyner's movement now brought his eyes around, for Koyner leaned forward, letting the forelegs of the chair thump against the floor as he came out of his seat. Koyner had made his decision in that split second. This was the time to get rid of Lonnigan.

SEVENTEEN

RAN LONNIGAN knew that he was in trouble. He had seen too many fights in the mountain saloons and behind the small schoolhouses after dances not to realize what he was up against.

He was caught in the middle of the floor, and he had no idea who was behind him. He glanced at the poker table. Mars Jacobs sat directly across from him. He had shoved his chair back when Jocko first flung the cards to the table top, but otherwise he had not moved.

The other two players were small merchants. Both wore black business coats and neither had a gun showing. Lonnigan turned a little and caught the half-breed's movement from the corner of his eye and spun, more afraid of the long-bladed knife than he was of Koyner's gun.

Jim Koyner chose this moment to make his move. His hand dropped to his side, resting on his gun, and he called softly, "Over here, Lonnigan. Over here." He meant to draw and shoot as the boy turned, but he counted without Mars Jacoby.

Jacoby had seen exactly what was going to happen and his own gun was out of its holster, the heavy barrel resting on the table edge, pointing directly at Koyner's stomach.

"Stop it," Jacoby said.

Koyner hesitated and in that instant Lonnigan took three side steps and swung around, his own gun in his hand. He no longer had the Indian at his back, but stood quartered to him.

"I said, stop it." Jacoby raised his gun a little from the table, the heavy barrel frowning at Koyner. "Call off your damn breed, Jim."

Koyner unwillingly took his eyes away from Lonnigan. He stared at Mars Jacoby and for a moment he came as near hating a man as he had ever done in his life. He seldom allowed himself the luxury of emotional feeling, but he also could never stand to be crossed, and Jacoby was crossing him now.

He stared into the mine owner's hard eyes and the conviction grew in his nimble brain that Jacoby meant exactly what he said, that Jacoby would no more hesitate in pulling the trigger than he would in stepping on a rattlesnake.

It was not physical fear which stopped Koyner. It was rather the knowledge that if he stopped Jacoby's bullet, all his careful planning would come to naught, and the uselessness of losing everything simply because of a casual barroom fight did not appeal to his sense of grandeur.

James Koyner was a man who, ever since childhood, had lived with the conviction that everything he did must be on a large scale. It had made him impatient with the slow, plodding progress which would have been his had he turned his talents to legitimate trade.

He had sought crime systematically, but only as a stepping-stone toward power. And when he died he hoped that he would go out in a blaze of notoriety, not in an obscure mountain saloon, in a town so small that it did not even boast a newspaper.

Elaborately, he holstered his own gun, saying as he did so, "Your pot, Mars. Put up the knife, Pete."

Indian Pete had been standing against the wall, his beady eyes taking in every motion in the room. At Koyner's command he slipped the knife into his belt, then as if he could not bear to be cheated of his prospective victim and still remain, he turned and moved quickly toward the saloon's front door.

Jocko Halleran chose this moment to groan and sit up. He glared at Lonnigan with red-rimmed eyes. It was obvious that no matter how the others felt, he still wanted to continue, but Koyner had had enough.

"Get up," he said. "Get your horse, and get out of here."

Halleran turned his head to stare at the outlaw leader, then he dragged himself to his feet with all the grace of a crippled grizzly and moved swayingly toward the door, nursing his wrist.

At the entrance he turned, conscious that every eye in the place was watching him, and said to Lonnigan in a tone which was loud enough to have carried halfway to the Division Point, "You'd better not be in the Junction when I ride in again." Then he went out, managing to swagger a little despite his hurts.

Jacoby was still seated. He was still holding his gun,

and it still pointed at Koyner. "Keep that man out of the Junction, Jim, or I'll see him at the end of a rope."

Koyner could brook no more. "Don't crowd your luck, Mars." His tone was vicious. "You won today. Let it rest."

"No." Jacoby was suddenly on his feet, moving with surprising quickness for one of his girth. And now the fight was no longer between Lonnigan and Koyner. It was between Jacoby and the outlaw, two strong men, both natural leaders who for three years had warily skirted each other's tracks.

"I've let you alone for three years." The mine owner's tone was low, but it carried an unmistakable warning. "I let you operate for reasons of my own, but that's finished. I don't want you in the Junction, and I don't want your men. It's your choice. Keep out of here, or I'll bring in the men from the ranches and hunt you down like coyotes. Now get out."

Koyner started to open his mouth.

"Get out." Jacoby's gun was steady, his purpose unmistakable.

Koyner went. He refused to hurry. He stalked the length of the long room with a kind of dignity which brought a feeling of admiration, even to Lonnigan.

Jacoby looked at his bartender. "See if they ride out."

The man behind the long counter obediently followed Koyner into the street. A minute later there was a rush of horses and a high-pitched yell which was Jocko Halleran's defiance to the town, then the bartender re-entered the saloon.

"They're gone."

Jacoby sat down, reholstered his gun. Now that the excitement was finished, he looked old and tired.

Lonnigan found that he was still holding his own gun and stuck it back into its place a little self-consciously. He did not quite know whether to thank Jacoby or not. In that country a man handled his own fights. He said, slowly and carefully, "You . . . you pulled me out of a bad hole."

Jacoby had actually forgotten him. Until that moment his full attention had been on Koyner. He knew that this was not the end of the story, but only a beginning. He turned now, his eyes focusing on the night operator.

"That's something I should have done a long time ago."

Lonnigan did not fully understand what Jacoby meant,

72

and that he could only maintain his leadership by decisive action, that Jacoby could no longer allow Koyner and his men to ride freely through the hills, that a battle was shaping up.

"They'll be back." Jacoby was speaking more to himself than he was to Lonnigan. "They may even be back tonight. Watch yourself. Halleran is a bad man with a grudge. Koyner cares nothing about you. Indian Pete has no feeling of any kind, but Halleran won't be able to live with himself as long as you are alive."

EIGHTEEN

CLYDE BULLOCK ordinarily went home at six. The superintendent was a man of fixed habits and ideas and it took a washout, a train wreck or a holdup before he voluntarily broke his rule, but on this night both he and Earnest were in the dispatcher's office, although Dix Dawson had the key.

For the news that the whole system had been waiting for had come through—the Japanese ship carrying the cargo of silk had docked at Seattle. The bales were already being transferred to the waiting train. The train would leave the terminal as soon as it was loaded and speed eastward, with rights against everything.

It should reach the Division Point sometime before midnight on the following evening, change crews and move on toward the plains.

Long ago Bullock and Earnest had worked out their careful schedule. Long ago they had picked the crews, they had selected the two engines and held them in readiness. And now the orders flashed up and down the line.

Sitting alone in the empty Junction station, Lonnigan read the messages as they flashed past and felt a kind of secondary excitement of his own.

The Silk Express was enough to catch the imagination of anyone. Freight being hauled in express cars, running at better-than-passenger time. The time for each division had been carefully worked out, and Bullock had frowned when he learned the exact schedule which the powers in Chicago had set up for him.

"If she holds the track," he'd told them grimly, "we'll put her through. If there is a failure, it won't be on the Mountain Division."

Brave words, but then Bullock felt a pride in his operation, a pride which was shared by most of his staff. He mentioned this now to Earnest and Dawson, ignoring January who sat as usual, writing orders.

January was long and thin and unattractive, with frog-like eyes which seemed about to pop from the yellow

74

mask of his face. A disappointed man—January—who hated the world and most of the people in it.

An hour later he slipped from the station and, crossing the tracks, made his way up Mountain Avenue to the Gold Run Saloon. Inside he paused at the bar, glancing a little thirstily at the rows of bottles which stood before the long mirror. Then he moved on back toward the poker tables at the rear end, catching Pinky Grimes's eye, walked on out through the rear door. Five minutes later Pinky emerged to find January waiting in the shadows.

"You took your time," he complained. "If Bullock misses me it's my neck."

Grimes was excited. His voice trembled slightly as his lips moved beneath his faded red beard. "The word?"

"The word is that the special runs through tomorrow night. I'd guess it will hit the Junction a little after nine o'clock. Let Koyner know, and remind him that the word comes from me."

Grimes was already moving away, headed for the livery stable. January stared after him, for one small instant half regretting his part in this. Then he muttered to himself, "If they'd used me right, I'd have been loyal." But he knew even as he said it that this was not the truth. He had never in his whole life been loyal to anyone, not even to himself. He hesitated for an instant, then with a feeling of bravado he turned back into the saloon and for the first time broke the railroad's cardinal rule. He had a drink while on duty.

With the whiskey sitting uneasily on his stomach, he turned back toward the station and was frightened as he came in through the waiting room to see that Bullock was standing by the bottom of the stairs talking to the master mechanic. January almost turned tail and fled, afraid that Bullock would see him, that the superintendent would smell the liquor on his breath. But he pressed by them, keeping as far away as he could, and scuttled up the steps like a scared rabbit, thankful that Bullock was so engrossed that he did not turn his head. With a sigh of relief January re-entered the dispatcher's office and slipped into his place.

If I don't get caught at this, he vowed to himself, I'll never, never do anything like it again.

Thirty-five miles away Lonnigan rose from the key

and peered out into the darkness beyond the tracks. He had heard movement which was not caused by the wind. An instant later he blew out the station lights and caught up the shotgun. Then Tracy McCable called, and he felt relief go through him.

The girl crossed the platform and came into the darkened station, saying as she thrust open the door, "I didn't mean to frighten you."

"I was just being careful." Lonnigan fumbled for a match, but she said quickly, "Why don't you leave the light off? If Halleran comes after you it will be better that way."

"Halleran?"

"I heard what happened in the saloon," she said, "and you were absolutely lucky that Mars Jacoby was there."

Lonnigan was offended. "I could have taken care of myself."

"You are," said Tracy McCable, "like all men. You think it is a disgrace to be helped by anyone. You would rather get yourself killed than admit that you need any assistance."

"Well," Lonnigan was still offended, "Uncle Charley always said . . ."

"I'm getting slightly tired of Uncle Charley and what he said," Tracy informed him. "I think it is about time that you started thinking for yourself."

Lonnigan wished that it were not quite so dark in the station. He wanted to see Tracy's face, for he had the uncomfortable sensation that she was laughing at him. But when she went on there was no hint of mirth in her voice.

"I don't like Jocko Halleran," she said. "He is the bad kind of Irish, and when they are bad there are none worse. He will nurse a grudge, and he will wait until he can catch you alone and in the dark, and then he will try to break you into small pieces."

"Two," said Lonnigan, "can play at that game."

"You are no match for Jocko Halleran," she told him.

"I don't know. I can shoot pretty well."

"It is not a matter of shooting. It is a matter of ruthlessness. Halleran is a ruthless man and therefore would have the advantage."

Lonnigan said, almost angrily, "You sound as if you admire him."

"I don't sound that way at all. I dislike and despise

76

Jocko and everything that he stands for. It is just that I don't want you hurt. I have other plans for you."

"You do?"

"I most certainly absolutely do," said Tracy McCable, "but I'm not ready to tell you yet."

She turned then and slipped from the door, and Lonnigan did not realize that she had gone until the door slammed behind her.

NINETEEN

LONNIGAN could hardly wait until Goodhue had entered the station on the following morning before he blurted out the news. "The Silk Express runs tonight."

Goodhue had not heard of the trouble in the Big Horn Saloon until he had gone off duty, for Lonnigan had not mentioned it. But everyone in town had been discussing Mars Jacoby's action in backing up the new night operator, and Goodhue had hurried down to give Lonnigan a warning.

"Never mind the silk special," he said without interest. "We knew that it would come through sometime this week. What's this I hear about you having trouble with Koyner's men?"

Lonnigan had been so full of the news that the silk train was to run at last that he felt deflated. "Why . . . why, it wasn't anything much. This Halleran must be crazy. I was just looking over his shoulder and he suddenly started to curse me."

Goodhue knew all about Jocko Halleran's superstitions and was not interested. What did interest him was Jacoby's apparent break with Jim Koyner. In this he saw a tiny ray of hope for himself. If Jacoby were serious, if he really ran the outlaw out of the territory, it would mean that Kate's affections might be freed.

The very thought brought a choking sensation into his throat. He visualized the girl as heartbroken by Koyner's departure, for he, more than anyone at the Junction, had guessed the depth of her feeling for the man.

And if she were heartbroken, she would need someone to talk to, someone who would understand. He pictured himself in this role, playing the sympathetic friend, listening to her grief, and gradually, ever so gradually, making her forget the outlaw.

It was a wonderful dream. Reason told him that it would not come true, but at the moment he had discarded reason.

"Tell me," he said eagerly, "just what did Jacoby do? Just what did he say?"

"Why?" Lonnigan was puzzled by the day man's interest. "He didn't say much. They had me in a jackpot, the Indian coming up on one side with his knife, and Koyner on the other with his gun. I could have gotten one of them, but I guess I'd have been in bad shape without Mr. Jacoby."

"But why did he do it?" This was what had puzzled Goodhue all morning. "Why did he decide to take your part?"

Lonnigan had not given this much thought, assuming that Jacoby had acted out of sheer decency. "Why, I guess he figured that the odds needed evening and . . ."

Goodhue shook his head. He felt that he knew Jacoby too well for that. He felt that Jacoby had moved because he had come to resent Koyner's attentions to his daughter, and in this he was nearly right, for Mars Jacoby had decided even before the trouble in the saloon that Koyner must go.

What he had hoped to learn from Lonnigan was whether Jacoby had mentioned this to the boy. Apparently Lonnigan had not the slightest idea what it was all about.

"Go on and get your breakfast," he said, almost roughly. "And if you'll take my advice, which you won't, you'll keep a weather eye out for Jocko Halleran. He's mean, and he'll stop at nothing to wipe out the fact that you knocked him down."

Lonnigan started to say that he had already been thoroughly warned, then as Goodhue turned away he realized that the station agent had little interest and, shrugging, reached for his jacket.

He came out onto the rear platform facing the yards and paused to look across the tangled tracks before following the covered walkway to the lunchroom.

The morning air was fresh and colder and it seemed that there was a smell of coming snow, blending with the scent from the pines and the coal smoke which always lingered around the station.

The upper yards were fairly deserted, but the loaded material cars in the lower yard almost cut off the view of the labor shanties.

The work train, with steam already up, stood chuffing on the Y-track as if impatient to begin its long climb to the bridge site above. The rusting boiler made popping sounds, and steam leaked at every ill-jointed connection

79

as the smoke eddied from the bell stack to further perfume the air.

Already the laborers were aboard, crowded into the two open-end coaches behind the loaded flatcars, waiting with the placid tolerance of recently fed cattle while the engine crew dallied as usual over breakfast in the lunchroom.

Lonnigan looked longingly at the train. He would much rather have run the engine than gone up to his bunkroom, but he needed sleep. Someday, he thought, he would bum a ride up to the new bridge site and watch the crew at work.

The train had been backed deep onto the Y-track so that only half a hundred yards separated the end of the rear coach from the inadequate stop at the track's end, and the thought crossed Lonnigan's mind that a heedless hand on the throttle could easily send the train rolling backward to dump itself into the thirty-foot canyon.

And then the shadow of movement beyond the wheezing engine caught his attention and he started forward as he saw a small boy scramble up into the gangway from the far side.

He knew exactly what was going to happen, since he too had the desire to operate an engine and he was running before the unheeded warning burst from his lips.

He vaulted forward, racing across the network of switching tracks toward the work train. The ties were slippery with morning damp and he stumbled twice. But he ran on, spurred by the startled cries from the laborers in the old coach as the train began to back.

Even as he caught the hand rail and swung up, he knew that it would be close. He had a glimpse of the boy's frightened face, the huge dark eyes that were already filling with tears, then he brushed the boy aside, reversing the old drivers with one hand while he used the other to dump the sand. Even as he did so he thanked the curiosity which had led him to hang around the switch engines at the Division Point during the days while Dawson was letting him work the key at night.

The drivers responded, but he felt the sickening, sliding, slithering motion as the momentum of the backing train carried them along the wet rails despite the spinning wheels. Then the drivers hit the sand and the train lurched to a jolting stop.

For an instant after he cut the throttle Lonnigan stood

perfectly still, conscious of the moisture beading his forehead. Then the boy tried to scramble from the cab, and Lonnigan caught him by the back of his loose overalls.

"Wait a minute." He pulled the boy to him. "Do you realize that you could have put the train into the canyon?"

The boy was trying to get free, whimpering as he struggled. "I'd have stopped it. I'd have stopped it."

"Not in time," said Lonnigan.

"But Jocko said . . ."

"What?" Lonnigan jerked him around. "You mean Jocko Halleran? What did he have to do with this?"

The boy was hardly ten, and very frightened. "He gimme a dollar. This morning he gimme a dollar. I wasn't to tell. He don't like the engineman. He said the crew shouldn't eat breakfast so long."

Lonnigan stared. The boy was obviously telling the truth. After a moment Lonnigan said slowly, "All right. Don't tell anyone else." Then he swung to the ground, taking the boy with him.

The yard was filled with running people. The laborers who had jumped to safety were picking themselves up along the track. The crew had charged from the lunchroom and were racing forward, but Tracy McCable had a head start and reached them first.

She dropped to her knees and pulling the crying boy from Lonnigan's grasp, comforted him. "It's all right, little Tony. I won't let them hurt you. I won't. I won't."

The crew boiled up, and as they arrived the women from the labor shanties came piling around the train. "Let me have that kid." It was the engineer. "I'll skin him alive. I'll teach him never to climb into my cab again." He made a grab for the boy, but Tracy McCable pulled him hastily out of the man's way.

"You let him alone, Ken Swansen! He didn't mean any harm. Every boy wants to run an engine."

Swansen made a grab for little Tony's ragged collar, but Lonnigan knocked his arm away. "That's enough. You heard what Tracy said."

The engineman swung to face Lonnigan. He was tall and thin, and his cheeks had a sunken look behind the drooping ends of his yellow mustache, but he was belligerent. "Keep out of this."

Lonnigan shook his head. "I'm in it. If it hadn't been for me your train would be in the canyon. Next time maybe you won't leave a fired-up engine standing alone while you loaf over breakfast."

Swansen's fireman and the labor foreman pushed up on either side of Lonnigan. The fireman was short and squat and powerful. The foreman was tall, a sad-faced Irishman with a broken nose and a wicked mouth.

"Maybe you want trouble?"

Lonnigan's whole manner underwent a subtle change. He had not been ready for an attack in the saloon the night before, but he was ready now. His mouth tightened and he reached out suddenly, catching the fireman by his belt and by the front of his sweat-stained shirt. He lifted him clear of the ground and threw him directly into the arms of the labor foreman. They went down together, cursing, a tangled mass of arms and legs, knocking the engineer sidewise as they fell.

"My," said Tracy McCable, to no one in particular. "Oh, my." No one else said anything. No one else moved. The foreman freed himself first, coming up and taking a partial step forward.

Lonnigan twisted to face him, one hand hanging in a loose fist at his side, the other thumb hooked in his sagging cartridge belt not far from the holstered gun. The foreman looked at the steady gray eyes, then let his eyes fall away to the hand close to the gun.

The foreman was not a coward. Armed with nothing but a pick handle, he had cowed twenty rebellious hunkies only the week before, but in Lonnigan's utter stillness his trained fighter's mind read a latent danger. He stood motionless for a full second, then he stooped and helped the fireman to his feet. The engineer turned away without a word, climbing up into the cab, and the spell was broken by the labor foreman as he raised his voice to a bellow, ordering the hunkies back into the coaches.

As if the words released them, the shanty women pressed in, and one shawl-clad figure jerked little Tony from Tracy's arm and, grasping his ear, led him away squalling.

The angry fireman followed the engineer into the cab, and Tracy, as she straightened, caught her high heel in a switch frog and would have fallen had not Lonnigan put out a quick hand to steady her. Then the hand was seized violently, and a heavy kiss was planted on the back. Instinctively Lonnigan snatched it free and turned to stare down into two of the largest, most liquid black eyes he had ever seen.

The eyes belonged to a squat Italian who could not have been an inch over five feet, but his body was powerful and his heavy lips were parted to show an even set of white teeth.

"My friend," he was babbling in excitement. "You save my boy. You save us all. Tony no forget."

Lonnigan was too surprised to answer, and a moment later the engineer saved him the trouble by tugging viciously on the cord. The whistle shrilled and the drivers of the old teakettle spun, starting the work train with a jerk. There were cries from the jabbering laborers who were still trying to get back aboard as they tumbled over one another in their hurried efforts.

Tony had calmed down somewhat. He grinned at Lonnigan, doffed his broken hat to Tracy McCable in a gesture worthy of a courtier, turned, and with no apparent effort, vaulted to the deck of the moving flatcar. There he stood, waving his hat and grinning widely as the old engine huffed its battered train out of the yards and took the new cut-off tracks toward the bridge site above.

"Well," said Lonnigan aloud. "Things can really happen rapidly at the Junction."

"You are a little hasty yourself upon occasion," said Tracy McCable. "I thought that O'Hara would beat you up. He is noted for beating people up—especially with a pick handle."

"He probably forgot his this morning."

She shook her head. "He saw something which I have probably missed. You have some war blood in your veins which I hadn't counted on."

Lonnigan's ears turned a faint red. He was already becoming embarrassed at the thought of his action. "I didn't need to be so rough," he admitted.

"You did," she told him. "You are a young man of untried force in a world where force is a real necessity."

"If you wouldn't use so many big words," he complained, "I might have more idea what you are talking about."

"I use big words because I like them," said Tracy, "and because they confuse people. I find it very expedient at times to confuse people."

In spite of himself Lonnigan laughed. "You're a funny person. I never knew anyone like you."

"I told you before that I am unique."

Lonnigan looked around, surprised to find that they were alone. The workers' wives were already halfway across the yard, herding their collective children in the direction of the string of shanties.

Terry McCable was standing at the lunchroom kitchen door, and Dan Goodhue was in the middle of the rear platform. As Lonnigan looked, both turned and disappeared into their respective buildings, figuring that the excitement was over.

"Well," said Tracy McCable. "At least you have made one friend at the Junction. That was Tony's son who started that engine."

"So I judged."

"And Tony will not forget." She looked at him steadily. "Nor is it wise to discount Tony's possible assistance. He is a kind of leader among his own people, and he would go through both fire and water for you."

"I have no intention of going through either fire or water." Lonnigan was grinning.

"A person never knows," Tracy said, "when they may be called upon to go through anything."

"You talk like you came out of a book," he complained.

"My mother was an actress," she said, "and she was educated, and she educated me, but she said that I had too many freckles to ever make a success on the stage."

He laughed again, then he sobered. "You know, I don't get it."

"Get what?"

"That boy, Tony. He said that Jocko Halleran gave him a dollar to start that train."

"He told you that? When?"

"In the cab. Now why would Jocko want to wreck that train?"

Tracy was silent, considering. "Halleran," she decided, "is a strange man with a twisted mind. You can't judge him by the standards of others. Maybe he has a girl among the labor-shanty women. Maybe he is angry with one of the workers who was on the train, maybe he merely thought it a joke for fifty men to be killed in the canyon, or maybe he did it on Koyner's orders."

Lonnigan stared at her. "But why would Koyner . . . ?"

"Why did they throw that rock at you through the station window? Answer that, and you will have answered many things."

84

TWENTY

FROM THE WINDOW of the lunchroom Tracy McCable watched Lonnigan leave the station and walk up the Junction's main street. It was late afternoon and she had not seen anything of him since that morning. She guessed that he had slept most of the day, but she could not understand why he had not come in for lunch and she wondered why he was going uptown. Perhaps, she thought, he was hoping for a sight of Kate Jacoby, and a small stab of jealousy made her frown.

I'm better than she is, Tracy thought. I'm smarter and nicer, and I'm not so bad-looking when I'm all dressed up.

Her father had been watching her from behind the counter and he said suddenly, "Stop worrying about him, Tracy girl."

She swung around, knowing that her color had heightened. "McCable," she said, "you mind your own business."

"It is my business." His tone was stubborn and she guessed at once that somehow, somewhere, he had secured a drink. "He's just an ignorant cowboy, and not good enough for the likes of you."

"The likes of me," she said and her tone was scathing. "And who are we to hold ourselves so proud? Where'd you get it, McCable?"

"Where did I get what?" He was all innocence.

"The drink." She headed toward the kitchen. "When I find it I'll pour it out—every drop."

Her father showed no signs of worry; then she knew that he had already drained the bottle and stopped. "Come on, where did you get it? Where did you get the money? What have you stolen this time?"

McCable drew himself up to his full height in offended dignity. "My own daughter, calling me a thief. I stole nothing. A gentleman gave me a small bottle."

"What gentleman?" She was more suspicious than ever. "There are no gentlemen in the Junction."

85

"If you must know," he said, "It was Jocko Halleran, and at least Jocko is Irish no matter what his other faults."

"The more shame to our race." She said it automatically for her brain was busy. Why should Jocko Halleran give her father anything? She turned and stiffened, for Jim Koyner was riding up the railroad track, followed by Halleran and Indian Pete.

They dismounted opposite the lunchroom and, leaving the breed to hold the horses, Koyner and Halleran crossed the tracks and thrust open the lunchroom door.

Tracy took a step to meet them. She admitted to herself that she was afraid of these men, but she was more afraid for her father. "What do you want?"

Koyner smiled. He had an easy way with all women and he could not see that Tracy was any different from any other. "Is that the way to talk to your best beau?"

Jocko Halleran giggled. Jocko had been drinking and he could not handle liquor much better than could McCable. Tracy was furious, wishing that she had worn her gun.

"Get out of here."

"This," said Koyner, "is a public lunchroom. Besides, I didn't come to see you, darling. I came to talk business with your father." He brushed by her and walked over to the counter, pulling a pint bottle from his pocket. "Have a drink, McCable."

Terry's eyes glistened, but he looked uneasily at Tracy and Koyner saw the look. Without turning he said to Halleran, "Put the girl in the storeroom."

Tracy was really frightened. She tried to duck past Halleran, but the outlaw was too quick for her. He caught her by the wrist, drew her toward him and wrapped his big arms about her slight body, then effortlessly he lifted her and carried her around the counter and into the kitchen. McCable moved convulsively and suddenly found himself looking into Koyner's gun.

"Steady," Koyner's voice was soft. "We won't hurt her. We just want her out of the way for a couple of hours. She can sleep on your bed in there, and she won't smother. Have a drink."

McCable looked at the gun, then picked up the bottle, pulled the cork, wiped the neck on his sleeve and drank deeply.

Halleran came back after having snapped the storeroom

86

lock into place. "She's safe," he said, and turned his too-bright eyes on McCable.

The liquor was warming McCable, mellowing him. Koyner was still holding the gun, but it no longer pointed directly at McCable's middle. "You're a thief," said Koyner pleasantly, "a petty, no-good thief, but we're going to give you a chance to make some real money. We're going to hold up that special silk train tonight."

The shock of the news partly sobered McCable. "And you're going to help us," Koyner added.

McCable wiped his slick mouth with the back of one trembling hand. "No."

"Yes," said Koyner, "unless you are a fool."

"You're the fool." McCable was staring at him. "What could you do with a cargo of silk in the middle of these mountains?"

Koyner's smile widened. "It's all arranged. Jocko has been in Mexico for the last month setting it up. Any fool can hold up an express car and take a few dollars, but silk—what will we do with silk?" He pretended to think. "I have it; we'll back the train up the new cutoff to the bridge site. We'll unload the silk and hide it in one of the abandoned mines and then in six months, a year—whenever the Pinkertons stop searching for it—we'll haul it down the outlaw trail and send it to Europe from Mexico. We already have our agents set up."

McCable wet his lips. The liquor he had drunk was already making his brain fuzzy. "What . . . what will the silk be worth?"

"Half a million," said Koyner, savoring the words, "three-quarters of a million—who knows. But there'll be plenty so that your share will give you more money than you ever had in your miserable life."

McCable's eyes lighted, and then they turned cunning. "It's a good plan," he said, "but why do you need me? Tell me that, Jim Koyner. Why do you offer me a share?"

"Not because I love you," said Koyner with real candor, "but because I need you. Our plan is very simple. We'll run out the night operator and have Chad Crawford take over his key. This Silk Express will have rights over everything, and Crawford will listen in to the train orders. As soon as the Express is reported out of Falling Leaf we'll cut the wires to the east and set the board against the train. The engineman won't want to stop, but he will, and you will be standing on the platform to tell him that there has been a slide in Paradise Canyon."

McCable was still frowning. "Why me?"

"Because," said Koyner, "Burke is on the engine. He will be suspicious of the stop, and we want to get him out of the cab without trouble. We don't want him to try to make a run for it. If Crawford shows himself Burke will smell something because he thinks that Crawford is dead, but there would be nothing odd about you standing on the platform, nothing odd about you knowing about the slide. He'll swing down and go into the station for orders. We'll grab him then. Think. For five minutes' work you can make twenty-five thousand dollars at the least."

McCable still hesitated. "But Burke will know I was in on the deal. He'll tell them . . ."

"You ride south with us," said Koyner. "Wouldn't you like to go back to Ireland with enough in your pocket to set yourself up as a gentleman? Here, have another drink."

McCable had another drink. Koyner turned to Halleran, saying in a low tone, "Give him just enough to keep him agreeable, and stay hidden in the kitchen. If he makes a wrong move, kill him."

He turned without another word and left the lunchroom, remounting and riding back up the track the way he had come, Indian Pete leading Halleran's horse. From the bay window Dan Goodhue watched them with a puzzled frown.

TWENTY-ONE

RAN LONNIGAN had gone uptown to the Big Horn in the hope of seeing Mars Jacoby, but the mine owner had spent most of the afternoon with one of his ranch foremen in the small office he maintained over Benson's store.

Lonnigan lingered, watching the poker game. It was cold outside, a chill wind sweeping down the canyon which warned of snow, and he did not return to the street until the early darkness reminded him that it was time to eat his evening meal if he were to be ready to relieve Goodhue at the station.

He stepped through the bat-wing doors and stood for a moment on the broken boards of the sidewalk, looking up and down the street, and there was enough light remaining of the gloomy day to let Kate Jacoby see him plainly.

She stood beside the front window in the yet unlighted hotel lobby and watched him for a full minute before she turned back to face Jim Koyner who lounged unconcerned in one of the cane-bottomed chairs.

"I tried to get Dad to ride out to the North Ranch for the night," she said, "but he wouldn't go. He said it was going to snow."

"Hope it does." Jim Koyner stretched his arms wide. "Snow will make things perfect, cover our tracks. And stop worrying about your father. I've enough men to control the whole town and I don't think Mars will take a hand. He hates the railroad."

"You never know what he will do." She looked at Koyner, wondering how he could take things so very easily. For herself, she was forced to keep fighting down her rising excitement. This was the night for which they had planned, the night that would bring them success or failure. The plan to hold up the silk train had seemed so simple when Koyner had first mentioned it, but she realized that all their actions had to be perfectly timed, that one slip . . . but there could be no slips. Everything was prepared for . . . She paced restlessly back to the window and watched Lonnigan's long form as he went down the street toward the station.

Something about him disturbed her. He was not like the other night operators who had been hazed away from the station. They would handle him, of course. She suspected that Koyner planned to kill him when the time came, and she did not care, but she wished that he had run. If he had only had the sense to run away . . .

But Lonnigan was not thinking of running as he crossed the tracks and entered the lunchroom. He was thinking of Tracy and wondering if she would be willing to wait at the station in order to see the Silk Express go by.

The running of a freight, on a faster than passenger schedule, had captured Lonnigan's imagination. Dan Goodhue had shown almost no interest and no one else in the mountain town seemed to be even aware that the train existed.

But Tracy, he felt, would appreciate the drama of the situation even if they would only see the cars for a minute as they raced by the Junction's platform. He pushed open the lunchroom door and looked around. The place was empty, but a moment later the kitchen door swung open and Terry McCable appeared.

Lonnigan realized as soon as he saw McCable that the man had been drinking, although he was not completely drunk, and he asked as he sat down at the counter, "Tracy around?"

"She went up to the hotel."

Lonnigan knew a quick feeling of disappointment. "Coming back tonight?"

McCable shook his head. He was not a good actor, and he was very afraid of Jocko Halleran who stood just inside the kitchen door with his gun drawn.

"You want steak?"

Lonnigan nodded, and McCable disappeared almost at once. Lonnigan stared after him, wondering what he should do. He knew that McCable's drinking would distress Tracy and he almost rose and went into the kitchen in search of McCable's bottle. Then he decided that after all it was not his business and he had no right bursting in. This decision saved his life, for Jocko Halleran was still standing just inside the door, his finger inching on the trigger. He would have killed Lonnigan where he sat at the counter had not he feared that the shot might be

90

heard and ruin their plans for the holdup by bringing the townspeople to the station.

McCable was nervous when he returned with the hot platter and steaming cup of coffee, but Lonnigan put the man's shaking hands down to the effects of liquor. He ate quickly and fifteen minutes later he walked into the station to relieve Goodhue.

The day man already had his hat on and was glancing at his watch. Lonnigan said in some surprise, "Don't you even want to stay down and watch the special pass?" Goodhue looked at him and the tart retort which was forming on his lips died. Instead he said, "Keep your enthusiasm, boy. You'll need it if you stay railroading," and, turning, stepped out into the cold chill darkness.

The wind had risen, sweeping down the street in small irregular gusts which caught up dust and trash in miniature whirling cones and slammed them against the unpainted sides of the board buildings. The station windows rattled and the stove choked on its own smoke, sending out bluish puffs around the top lid and through the bent joints of the pipe.

Lonnigan coughed and moved over to look at the sheet. He noted that the whole western end of the Division had been cleared between eight and nine. Bullock was taking no chances; if the special were running ahead of time he meant to let Burke save every minute that he could.

The sounder chattered and Lonnigan sat down at the table. He had forgotten the Greening which stood in the far corner. His whole attention was on the messages flashing back and forth across the wire.

And then Darcorte reported the Silk Express in sight. Darcorte was the furthest station west which came under the Mountain Division. Lonnigan read Dawson's orders to the operator. He heard the operator report. The Silk Express was in and out at six-o-one, seven minutes ahead of time.

But Burke would lose that on the rising, twisting grades. If he made the Division Point on time Bullock would be more than satisfied.

Elmhurst reported the train in and out at six-thirty-five, and it was twenty-nine miles from Darcorte to Elmhurst. Burke was holding it to almost a mile a minute, but he was losing a little as the grade steepened and the tangents tightened. It was like watching a puzzle, seeing each piece drop into place. Lonnigan was so intent that he did not hear the noise outside above the gust of the wind.

His first warning was the bullet which shattered the glass above his head. Fortunately for him, it struck the swinging lamp and threw the station into darkness. Lonnigan dropped, unconsciously reaching for the shotgun which wasn't there. Then he turned and crawled hurriedly toward the stairs.

TWENTY-TWO

OUTSIDE THE STATION all was quiet as Lonnigan scuttled across the floor toward the foot of the stairs; then a voice shouted, "All right, Lonnigan. The place is surrounded. Come out with your hands up."

It sounded like Koyner's voice, but the wind was gusting so that he could not be sure. He went up the stairs at a crouching run, crossed the bunkroom and slid out onto the sharp pitch of the roof, having sense enough to pull the window down behind him.

It was cold and he had not stopped to grab his jacket. He shivered as he turned and moved across the rough shakes of the roof, careful to stay below the ridge so that his body would not be outlined against the lighter sky. But he did crawl to the crest and peer over.

In the darkness it was hard to tell how many men there were below, but he heard them shifting about and thought that he saw horses in the shadows beyond the tracks.

Then he heard Koyner say, "Two of you go in after him. We'll cover you through the window."

This, he thought, was different from the other attacks. This was not a warning. His guess was confirmed a moment later as he heard Jocko Halleran's grumbled words, "Let me go in. The bullet in my gun was made for that squirt."

He moved along the roof then, knowing that it was only a matter of minutes, perhaps seconds, before they discovered that he was no longer in the station. He glanced at the tangle of tracks in the switching yards and as he did so, he saw the headlamp of the work train coming down the grade from the dam site.

Immediately below him there was a sudden argument, and his heart leaped. With the work crew coming in, Koyner's men would undoubtedly scatter. But in this he was wrong. As the engine pulled into the yard he saw a number of dark figures steal forward across the tracks.

The old engine chuffed to a stop. The labor foreman dropped off, threw the Y-track switch and the engine reversed, pushing the old coaches back onto the Y. The train had not stopped moving when the workers began to drop off, heading directly away from the station toward the labor shanty row.

Then the engineman and his fireman stepped down to be joined by the labor foreman and they started across to the lunchroom. They never made it. From behind the dark cars Koyner's men were suddenly around them. Lonnigan heard the engineer curse, heard a blow struck, and then the fireman's whining tones.

"What's the idea? What's the idea?"

"Lock them in the baggage room." It was Koyner. "Come on, Halleran. Halleran, did you find that night operator?"

There was a curse from the station door. "He ain't in here."

"He's got to be. Look upstairs, you fool."

For the moment Lonnigan had forgotten his own predicament, but Koyner's words recalled it to him and he looked around. Now there were lights in every direction as lanterns flared. Koyner had not lied; the station was truly surrounded.

And then his eye caught the long roof, which covered the walkway to the lunchroom, and he crawled toward it, keeping as flat against the shakes as he could.

The walkway roof was not as steeply pitched as was the station's and he traversed it quickly, still crouched so that his head did not show above the gable, and did not pause until he was over the lunchroom.

Lights had now flared inside the station and streamed from the gable windows of the bunkroom. He wondered how soon the searchers would think to look for him on the roof. He had to get off it as fast as possible.

But Koyner's men were fanned out clear across the yards. If he dropped down he would be seen at once. He was like a treed animal, held at bay by a set of quartering hounds, and then his hand touched the edge of the ventilator and he froze.

It was merely a square pipe of tin which extended two feet above the even line of the roof with a weather shield across its top, held in place by clamps. This he removed without difficulty, spurred on by the shouts of the searchers below as they hunted him.

Two inches below the top of the pipe was a screen. He pulled his long knife and managed to pry down beside the shield and found that the screen was merely set in place, resting on a half-inch collar.

He raised one end enough to get his fingers under it and carefully lifted it out. Then he risked a friction match, holding it at arm's length down the pipe so that the flame could not be seen by the men in the yards below him.

Less than five feet down the pipe he saw the rounded metal hood which covered the stove and the square opening which led into the vent. It would be easy enough to lower himself to the stove if his shoulders would go down through the pipe.

There was still fire in the stove. The heat came up around him and he had the momentary thought that if he stuck he might well hang there until he fried. The pipe felt tight about his shoulders, but he raised his arms and managed to wiggle down until his feet hit the stove.

He squatted quickly and jumped to the floor before his boot soles would burn through, and in doing so he knocked over a pan that had been resting on the stove. It fell with a crash in the darkness.

He crouched motionless, his hand dropping to make certain his holstered gun was still in place. It seemed to him that the searchers out in the yards could not have avoided hearing the crash, but as he listened he heard nothing but a steady thumping. He held his breath, trying to decide what it was. It could be one of the searchers pounding on the outside lunchroom door, but it seemed closer, much closer than that.

And then he thought of the storeroom and it flashed through his mind that Tracy must have returned, found her father drinking and locked him in the storeroom.

He chanced another match to locate the door and the heavy lock, then the faint flare showed him the key glittering on a nearby shelf, and he hastily unlocked the door. His idea was to quiet the drunken man so that McCable's pounding would not draw attention to them. He never thought of Tracy until she stumbled out into his arms.

"Ran."

The match he had been holding in his free hand burnt his fingers and he dropped it, leaving them in darkness. "Shh."

"What is it?" she said in a whisper. Her small hands were on his shoulders.

95

"Koyner's gang," he told her. "They ran me out of the station. I sneaked across the roof and came down through the ventilator. How'd you get into that store-room?"

"Koyner put me there. He came and got my father drunk. They're up to something."

"What?"

Again Tracy hated to admit that she did not know. She moved over to the kitchen window and peered out. Half a dozen lanterns bobbed across the switchyards as Koyner's men searched around the cars.

"Eventually they'll think of looking here," Tracy said. "You've got to get out of here. I know! I'll dash out the front door yelling. That'll bring every man from the yards on the run."

"No," said Lonnigan.

"Yes," Tracy informed him. "Don't be an absolute, utter idiot and think that just because you are a male you are superior. Jim Koyner isn't going to kill me. He wouldn't dare. If it got around the mountains that he had harmed a woman the boys from the mines and ranches would hang him from a tree." She turned in the darkness and moved toward the swinging door. "When you hear me yell unfasten the rear door and run across the yards to Tony's shanty. It's the last one on the row." She came back and fumbled around the sink. "Darn it."

"What's the matter?"

"My gun is gone. McCable must have taken it."

"Wait." Lonnigan put out a hand to stop her, but she brushed past him in the darkness. "Remember, when I yell you dash. And you wait until you hear from me. Don't go around in the dark playing hero. Koyner has got more than twenty men."

"Wait, I said . . ." Lonnigan heard the swinging door creak and jumped forward, but he was too late. Tracy was already halfway across the lunchroom.

"You can't stop me." Her whisper carried clearly, and a moment later he heard her rattling the heavy bolt, then her shout split the night.

"Koyner! Jim Koyner? What do you mean by having me locked up?"

There was a shout in answer, then the rush of feet as the outlaws ran around the building. He heard the girl scream, he heard McCable curse, and then he heard Koyner shouting orders to his men and waited for no more.

He eased the rear door open, peered along the rear platform, found it deserted and crossed it with a bound, hitting the loose ballast of the switchyard and racing across it to the first line of shadowy freight cars.

He jumped over the coupling between two cars, and stopped in their shelter for a moment to survey the ground ahead. Behind him the night was a confused bedlam of shouts, but ahead everything looked clear.

He stole forward now, his gun loose in his hand and reached the work train that now sat abandoned on the Y-track. As he rounded the engine he saw the dark shape of a man in the faint light from the distant stars. He halted at once, calling, "Koyner wants you. They found him," and watched the man start to run toward him, and was ready with his swinging gun.

The man went down without a sound as Lonnigan brought the long barrel down directly across the crease in his hat. He bent over to make certain that the man was out, and then moved forward toward the lower yard, crowded with its string of material cars, loaded with supplies for the new bridge.

Once among the cars he felt safer and stopped, looking back in the direction of the station. But the gusts of cold wind were coming steadily, and only the faint sound of men's shouts reached him.

He shivered. He was tempted to circle the yard and follow the canyon line where it came back to the station from the east, but already his teeth were beginning to chatter. The thing to do was press on to Tony's, to borrow a coat of some kind. If he stayed in the yards in his shirt sleeves he would freeze. He moved on then, coming along the row of shacks until he reached the end one and paused to hammer on the door.

For a full minute there was utter silence from within and he repeated the knock, using the barrel of his gun. "Come on, Tony, open up."

There was the sound of fastenings being withdrawn; the door opened a crack and an eye appeared. "What you want?"

"A coat," said Lonnigan. Then he realized that Tony did not recognize him. "Tracy McCable sent me."

"Ah!" The door came wide, throwing lamplight across Lonnigan's face and Tony recognized him. He reached out, seized Lonnigan's hand and pulled him in. "You are safe, my friend. I hear the noise from the station. I fear for you." He slammed the door and pushed Lonnigan into a small room already crowded by a woman and five small frightened children.

Outside the wind swooped with a renewed gust which threatened to overturn the small building.

TWENTY-THREE

THE FIRST WARNING of trouble that Clear Water had was when Dix Dawson failed to raise any of the stations beyond Paradise Canyon. Even then, it took minutes for the night dispatcher to associate the trouble with the Silk Express.

A storm was blowing up out of the northwest, one of the spring blizzards which could be so disastrous to the mountain country, and he thought that the winds might have carried the wires away.

He failed to make contact with Lonnigan at the Junction, but he merely assumed that the new night operator had been run away from the station by the ghost and even smiled slightly to himself.

Falling Leaf had reported Burke and the express in and out only two minutes late, and Dawson had settled back, relaxing, for, if he knew Paddy Burke, the engineman would bring the train into the Division Point ahead of time or blow a tube trying.

But a few minutes later Dawson put through a call to Indian Wells and realized suddenly that the wire was open. And still he did not worry. Habit of thought is a strong thing, and the wind had torn out their wire many times before.

The minutes ticked away and he called Falling Leaf again, getting no response. He began to curse then, for on occasion Dawson could be a profane man. He sent the call boy to Bullock's, for the superintendent had not gone home. The boy found Earnest, the master mechanic and the train master in Bullock's office and the three of them hurried down the hall, Bullock glancing at his watch as they came. The Silk Express was due in five minutes.

Dawson was still trying to raise the Junction, trying to raise Falling Leaf, trying to raise any station west of Paradise Canyon, and having no luck. He looked up, pushing back his eye-shade.

"Wind probably took the wires down, but where's the special? We ought to hear her by now."

Bullock moved over to the window which commanded a view of the track from the west. Below him the relay crew waited with a little group of railroad employees around them. Everyone was watching, waiting. The minutes dragged by, and still there was no rumble from the expected train. Five minutes went by . . . ten.

Dawson said to no one in particular, "Burke was only two minutes late out of Falling Leaf."

The silence settled over the room, the tension grew. The train was fifteen minutes late.

"Something's happened," Dawson said, unable to contain himself. "Burke would burn the boxes out of her to get in on time. And the wire—maybe it wasn't broken by the wind. Maybe someone cut it."

Bullock swung around from his place at the window. He looked more like a bear than ever as he came over to the table. "What are you trying to say? A cut wire would mean a holdup."

Dawson glared back at him. "We've had trains held up before."

Bullock's tone grated with impatience. "Talk sense. What would a gang of rag-tail outlaws do with half a million dollars worth of silk in the middle of the mountains?"

"Well," said Earnest, speaking for the first time, "where's the train?"

"I don't know." Bullock had no patience. "Maybe Burke threw a rod, maybe he had a hotbox, a hundred things could delay him, and if the wires are down he'd have no way of letting us know." He crossed to the table and, brushing Dawson aside, took over the key, calling Chicago.

Big Jim was in the Chicago office that night. Big Jim might be a promoter and a financial wizard but he also prided himself that he was an operator. He left the group of dignitaries and newspaper men who were standing by, waiting for news of the special, and took the key himself. Then he and Bullock talked back and forth across the miles of swaying wire.

Finally Chicago set up a loop and reached Indian Wells by way of the Union and the west coast. Indian Wells reported that they could raise nothing to the east of Falling Leaf, that apparently the wire was broken west of the Junction.

Time had passed. The special was an hour and a half

overdue at the Division Point. Earnest said, "I wonder what's happened to Lonnigan? I thought his story was too glib."

Bullock turned on him savagely. "What are you carping about now?"

"Well," said Earnest. "Figure it out for yourself. Koyner's outlaws or somebody has been running the night operators out of the Junction for almost six months. Then Lonnigan rides in with his cock-and-bull story. He admits to being mountain-bred. What's to prevent him from being one of the outlaws sent here as a plant?"

Bullock said nastily, "It was your idea to send him to the Junction, and he was attacked the first night he was there."

"Was he?" said Earnest. "How in the devil do we know that he just didn't report an attack to make things look good? The other operators were attacked and they ran. Lonnigan didn't run because his outlaw friends wanted him just where he was. It's all a part of the same plan."

Bullock stared at him, half convinced in spite of himself, but he voiced again the question which he had asked before. "What in the devil does any outlaw, Jim Koyner or not, intend to do with a whole trainload of silk in the middle of the mountains?" It was a question that none of them could answer, and no one tried.

The Chicago office was in worse turmoil than was the station at Clear Water. The Silk Express had been advertised so widely that it had become page one news for every paper east of the Mississippi. The story had captured the imagination of the American people. It had become a sporting event, a race against time, a renewed proof that men and equipment could beat the hazards of nature.

Big Jim paced back and forth across the office. His associates stared at each other in consternation. It was too bad that James Koyner was not there to see what his operations had done to the huge railroad. It would have pleased him and salved his pride that he, with some twenty men, could knock down the solid structure which had been built up. But Koyner was not there.

It was the road president who ordered out the wrecker. Big Jim had waited as long as he dared before he flashed the message to Bullock. But they had to do something. Until the lost train was located the whole Mountain Division was paralyzed.

101

Bullock turned away from the key, looking old and tired and curiously shrunken. No one was blaming him, and yet it was his division which had failed. He moved downstairs as the hissing locomotive and its two coaches pulled out from the passing track onto the main and watched the men scramble aboard, then Bullock climbed into the engine cab.

The coaches were loaded with what men the master mechanic could find, wipers from the roundhouse, switchmen out of the yards, together with the regular wrecking crew. Danny Shea was at the throttle and Fred Koble was firing for him.

Every man on board knew that they were in danger while moving against the lost Express and that any moment the missing silk train, unaccountably delayed, might come high-balling around one of the sharp tangents and plow into their head end. They were armed, since even Bullock now admitted the possibility of a holdup, but they were more fearful of a possible collision than they were of the outlaws.

No one realized the danger more than Bullock, and he stared fixedly at the twisting track as it unwound beneath their wheels. Half a dozen times some trick of the wind seemed to bring to their ears the rushing sound of another train. It had begun to snow, and the white flakes were driven directly into their faces, making it all but impossible to see.

Danny Shea, old and wise in the ways of the Mountain Division, eased the big engine along at a snail's pace, ready to reverse his drivers, ready to send his train scuttling crabwise in an effort to get into the clear if there were any sign of the missing Express.

But there was no sign. They reached the mouth of Paradise Canyon and started down the long descending grade, which at times ran on its shelf above the foaming water, at others actually hung from the steep face of the sheer canyon wall. They were running so slowly that a man could have dropped from the handirons and kept pace at a dog-trot had there been room for him between the train and the roaring river.

Bullock had no thought of dropping off. He peered ahead against the snow as the headlamp battled to cut its light through the blanketing darkness, and then Danny Shea suddenly cut the throttle.

"Hear something?"

The engineman braked the train. He wasted no time in answering, but swung out onto the cat walk and stepped surefootedly along the hot boiler to the front end. A moment later he turned and motioned Bullock forward with a swinging arm. "Come look."

Bullock came up, puffing a little in the thin, cold mountain air. He did not need Danny's words to understand. The spray of light from the headlamp showed him the wrecked bridge, the swirling river raging across the open gap, twisting over the broken girders and the stringing rails.

The bridge across the Devil's Cut was out and it had not gone out from natural causes. Someone had blown it to pieces. The Division Point was cut off effectively from the west end. Koyner, in planning his explosion, had chosen his spot shrewdly. Here the rails had crossed from the south to the north bank of the stream and there was no room to work in the V-shaped canyon, no room for a shoofly, no room for a temporary spur.

The material train with its crane would have to back clear out from the Division Point and the men would be working over themselves as they labored to replace the bridge. It would take hours, perhaps days, before the Mountain Division would roll again.

TWENTY-FOUR

PATRICK BURKE was a happy man. He loved speed, and on this night he was living an engineman's dream, piloting a train with absolutely no orders against it.

On the straight-of-way past Falling Leaf station he did not ease up as his wheels clattered over the switch frogs. He was two minutes late. The station lights flashed by and he had a fleeting glimpse of the night operator waving from the doorway as the six cars of the Silk Express swept past the platform. Then they hit the rising grade and he eased slightly for the first curve of the Dawson Cut. With luck, they should be in the Division Point in sixty minutes.

Burke had a momentary look at his fireman's sweaty face as the coal went in and the licking fire flamed. He glanced automatically at the gauge, noting his pressure, and then his eyes were back on the track where his swaying headlamp cut its white path through the darkness.

Up through the cut they ran, and over the looping curves that carried them across the divide, then downward into the canyon of the White Water and so into the Junction.

When he saw the board set against him Patrick Burke could not believe his eyes, but his action was instinctive as he cut the throttle and hit the brakes, so late that they nearly ran past the station.

They came to a puffing stop beside the yellow building, and, with anger burning in his soul at the lost seconds, Burke swung down out of the cab, searching angrily for the night operator.

And then he saw McCable standing on the platform and called harshly, "Has the operator lost his mind? What's that board doing against me?"

"Washout in Paradise Canyon." McCable was drunk, but not so drunk that he couldn't talk plainly.

Burke stopped to stare, and the crew from the train was already on the platform, crowding around him. "I'll see about this." The engineman swung toward the station door. It opened and he found himself staring into the gun that Jim Koyner held.

"Take it easy." Koyner was smiling. "This is a holdup."

Burke swore. He turned and had a vague idea of dashing back to the train, but Jocko Halleran had led the rest of the outlaws around the station and closed in on the startled crew. Burke tried to break through, and Halleran beat him to the platform with the barrel of his gun, grunting loudly with each downward stroke.

"Stop it." Koyner grabbed Halleran's arm. "Get them into the baggage room." He watched while the sullen crew was herded toward the baggage room where they joined the imprisoned men from the work train, then he turned and went into the office where Chad Crawford bent above the key, his scarred face intent.

"Everything okay?"

Crawford nodded. "Dawson is talking to the Falling Leaf operator. They don't suspect a thing."

Koyner grunted, "All right," and moved outside into the full light from the bay window, then he raised both arms in the prearranged signal.

Far down the track in each direction an outlaw on a telegraph pole saw the signal and used his cutters on the wire. They slid down from their perches and hurriedly moved to the next pole, then climbed it to cut a full section from the line. This wire they carried off into the brush. Koyner did not want the line repaired too readily. He turned when Halleran came back from locking the prisoners in the baggage room.

"Tell Joe to get going. I want that Devil's Cut bridge blown within half an hour." Halleran moved away, but Koyner called him back. "Any sign of Lonnigan?"

Halleran swore. "None at all."

"What happened to the McCable girl?"

"Indian Pete took her uptown. She's locked in the livery stable office."

Koyner nodded approval, then whirled sharply as he heard a rustling noise behind him. Terry McCable was standing there, so drunk by this time that he was swaying. His coat was open and flapping in the wind so that it exposed the heavy-bladed French knife thrust in his belt. He grasped the handle of the knife now.

"Koyner," he said, reaching out and putting a hand on Halleran's shoulder to steady himself, "release my daughter."

Koyner had no time for the lunchroom man and tried to brush by him, but McCable grabbed his arm. "You hear me?" He spoke with drunken insistence. "You release her, you hear?" Jocko Halleran settled McCable by knocking him flat.

TWENTY-FIVE

MARS JACOBY ate supper with his daughter in the hotel dining room. He noticed that she was nervous and that she kept glancing at the small watch she wore pinned to one shoulder of her ruffled shirtwaist.

In his own way, Mars Jacoby was a simple man and he reduced life to simple things. He judged that his daughter's agitation was caused by Koyner, and his resolve that the man should go crystalized. He would do something about it on the morrow.

He finished first and rose, nodding to a dozen people scattered in the room as he passed toward the door. He knew that they watched him, some with dislike, some with fear and none with true friendship.

He had never been a man who made friends. In his younger days the urge to succeed had held him slightly aloof from his fellows, and after success had come, there had been none to match him in this mountain country.

As he moved onto the wide porch he detected the smell of snow in the air and frowned at the thought of his scattered herds, already on the way to the higher hills for the approaching summer. A hard blizzard could hurt him badly, but there was nothing that he could do about it and, with the fatalism of a true gambler, he put it from his mind, descending the steps and walking over to the Big Horn.

The saloon was one of his lesser holdings, but he derived more real pleasure from it than from his ownership of anything else.

It was, in effect, his office and his club, all wrapped into one. It was the place where people found him, where messages were delivered from the ranches or the mines, and where he found his only recreation.

On this evening there were already four men at the poker table when he entered and he nodded to them as he slipped into the seat which was always left vacant for him. These four were regulars, and the game they played was for small stakes. There was Benson who ran the store, Haddock from the livery, Fischer who owned a small mine up the canyon and Dan Goodhue.

Goodhue was seated directly across the table from Mars Jacoby and he raised his eyes, giving the mine owner the barest of nods before dropping his attention back to the cards which he held fanwise in his small hands.

Jacoby looked around. The room was practically deserted. Another hour and it would be well filled, for it offered the only amusement that the town boasted.

Then Jacoby turned back to the table and watched Goodhue as the station agent gathered up the discarded cards and riffled them easily before dealing.

Goodhue had been in the Junction for nearly three years, a quiet man who minded his own business and who had never had trouble with anyone. Jacoby, despite his hatred of the railroad, had never felt any resentment against Goodhue. As he picked up the cards which Goodhue had dealt, a shot sounded from the lower end of the street.

Benson laughed. "Sounds like Koyner's men are hazing the new operator again. They're liable to get surprised. He bought some buckshot, and a shotgun can make one man the equal of several."

Jacoby glanced at Benson, thinking that Koyner had certainly established himself with the townspeople. Benson was honest and respectable, a typical example of the average merchant who was willing to wink at the activities of his customers as long as they did not affect him. Then he looked at Goodhue, wondering what the day agent was thinking about, but Goodhue's freckled face was as expressionless as if he had not heard the shot.

The game went on, time passing unnoticed by the players. Nor did the roar of an arriving train register on Jacoby until he saw Goodhue lay down his cards and pull out his watch.

And then suddenly Goodhue was on his feet, staring across the heads of the players to the door. "It stopped!"

Benson had a good hand and he was annoyed by the interruption. "So a train stopped. Is that anything out of the way?"

"It's the Silk Express." Goodhue was looking toward the doorway, then his eyes regarded those of the players and he became aware that not one man at the table comprehended what he was talking about.

"It's a special," he said, speaking half to himself. "It shouldn't stop anywhere this side of Clear Water. It wouldn't have stopped unless something has happened . . . It . . ." Apprehension flooded through him then. "The fools! They're holding it up. Koyner's holding up the silk train."

They stared at him, hardly understanding and not particularly concerned.

"I've got to go down there," Goodhue muttered vaguely, still standing there, uncertain, irresolute. To Jacoby, watching his face, it was obvious that the man was afraid.

"You're a fool," said Benson. "Keep away from there. Koyner will blow your head off." The force of the words had more effect on Jacoby than they did on Goodhue.

This was Jacoby's town, his country, and the idea that Koyner or anyone else would have the nerve to stage a holdup within the town limits was more than he could stand.

"I'll go with you." He pushed back his chair, coming to his feet. The other two players looked up at him, but made no move to follow, nor did Jacoby expect them to. He felt no personal fear, and the resentment that had been growing within him against Koyner would have blinded him in any case.

In his thoughts Jacoby felt that Koyner was getting too big for his britches. Through the years Jacoby had seen other men get too big and he had knocked them down, putting them in their places. That's what he meant to do with James Koyner.

He strode from the saloon, neither knowing nor caring that Goodhue followed. He reached the street, slamming the bat-wing doors out of his way with a gesture of his wide shoulders and turned down toward the railroad.

In the blaze of the station lights the stalled train was clearly visible, and the townspeople were out on the sidewalks staring down in its direction. But no one made any move to follow Jacoby and Goodhue as they passed. The years of acceptance had made them reluctant to oppose Koyner's men, as long as the attack was not turned on the town itself. Only then would they take part.

Both Jacoby and Goodhue ignored them, taking the center of the street, their boots roiling up little dust puffs which the wind caught and whipped away.

They reached the bottom of the street and circled the

standing train to come out at the end of the platform, turning to move toward the station.

There were a dozen outlaws on the platform, but Jacoby ignored them, for he had seen Koyner standing outside the station bay arguing with McCable, and he made directly for the outlaw chief stopping only when he was facing Koyner.

"You damn fool!" All the rage and irritation that he felt with the man came up into his voice. "What do you mean by stopping this train?"

Koyner had been ready for the meeting as soon as he had seen Jacoby appear around the end of the train. He was too shrewd not to have realized that sooner or later Jacoby and he would crash head-on, and he almost welcomed the opportunity. He made an unobtrusive hand signal to Jocko Halleran who had been lounging against the station wall watching his tilt with McCable, and Halleran's bearded lips split in their grin of understanding.

Koyner turned them, centering his attention on the mine owner as Jacoby came up. "Keep out of this, Mars." His tone told plainly that he did not care what Jacoby did. He gave Goodhue a cursory glance then ignored him, certain in his knowledge that the station agent was not dangerous.

"No," said Jacoby. "Put the engineer back on that train and send it on its way. If you don't, I'll call in my men from the hills and hunt you down like a dog."

Koyner laughed, and his laugh was echoed by Mc-Cable. The lunchroom man was still half drunk, but the obvious rage on Jacoby's face was pleasing to him as no liquor ever was.

"You're no longer top dog," he said. "You've shot your wad, Jacoby. No one pays attention to you any more."

Jacoby's rage sharpened at McCable's words, and he turned so that he faced the Irishman fully. "So you're in this too." His contempt was unmistakable. "I had you pegged as a petty thief. I didn't know that you were a turncoat and a traitor, a cheap informer who would sell out the people who employ you."

No other words Jacoby might have chosen could have had greater effect upon McCable. His grin vanished and the skin tightened over the hinges of his small jaw. His hand came down, seeking the French knife which he still wore thrust into the front of his belt. He drew it and raised the point of the heavy blade toward Jacoby.

110

Jacoby took a step backward and his gun was in his hand. "Drop that knife, you fool!"

Jocko Halleran chose that moment to shoot them both. His first bullet caught Jacoby directly in the heart. The mine owner was dead before he hit the platform. McCable saw him fall, and his dazed brain was too clouded to realize for an instant what had happened. Then Halleran's second bullet caught McCable in the small of the back, straightening him up with its powerful force and then sending him forward to fall, face down, shot directly through the stomach.

Goodhue uttered a half-strangled gasping cry and took a step as if to interfere, and Koyner knocked him senseless with a single blow to the chin. Then he turned, motioning to his substitute engineer.

"Let's get out of here. We've wasted too much time already."

TWENTY-SIX

THE TWO-ROOMED SHANTY which Tony, his oversized wife
and his five children occupied was hot and smelled of
too many bodies and too much cooked food.

Tony cleared a sagging bed by the simple expedient
of pushing two of his youngest from it to the dirt floor
and insisted that Lonnigan sit down.

Lonnigan hesitated, looking around. He wanted to get
a coat, and then he wanted to get out of there. Twelve
dark, mellow eyes watched him with frank intentness.
The eyes were not unfriendly, but even in Tony's look
he read a reservation which was put there by uncertainty
and fear.

These people were in a new land, a raw land, a ruthless land, without friends, without a full understanding
of the language or the customs of the people around
them.

The wife, squat and broad and work-worn, said something to Tony in Italian and he answered in the same
language, then he again motioned Lonnigan toward the
sagging bed. "You sit, please."

Lonnigan shook his head. "I want to borrow a coat.
Coat." He indicated his shirt sleeves. "It's cold. Then
I've got to find out what's going on."

"No go out," said Tony. "You get killed." He picked
up his broken hat. "I look. They no kill Tony."

Before Lonnigan could stop him the section man had
pulled open the door and vanished into the cold night.
Lonnigan started to follow, but the boy he had pulled
from the train that morning jumped between him and
the door.

"You wait," he said. "Papa say you wait."

Lonnigan waited with mounting impatience. He heard
the thunder of the approaching Express, and at the back
of his mind he realized it was the silk train. He thought,
I planned to stand on the platform and wave to Burke as
it goes by, and here I am cooped up because some of
Koyner's boys needed some exercise. He was getting

112

madder by the minute, and then he heard the train stop. For an instant he puzzled over it, and then he reached down without a word and lifted little Tony from his way, pulled the door open and rushed out into the night.

He could see the train drawn up at the station almost an eighth of a mile away, and he sprinted toward it, swearing softly under his breath. But he had not covered a quarter of the lower yard when his toe caught in a switch frog and he fell heavily, his head striking against an iron rail.

He lay there, not out, but too dazed to move. He could not be certain of how long he lay there, perhaps it was a minute, perhaps it was ten. It was the sound of two shots which brought him back to full consciousness. He struggled upward, fumbling for his hat which had fallen in the darkness. He found it and winced as he fitted it onto his head. There was a lump the size of a hen's egg above his right temple.

One shoulder ached and one hip hurt as he rose, and he was so chilled that his muscles did not seem to work right. He peered toward the station, and as he did so he saw the lights of the rear car move, apparently toward him.

He blinked his eyes, thinking for a moment that the bump on the head had affected his vision, then he realized that the Express was backing away from the station. He watched as it gathered speed, and then it came to him that the train wasn't backing up the main line but rather onto the cut-off which led to the bridge site in the mountains fifteen miles above.

He started to run again, cutting across at an angle, hoping to reach the train before it cleared the yards. But Koyner's engineer was wasting no time. The light train gathered speed with surprising rapidity, and Lonnigan was still a good hundred yards away from the spur, when the puffing engine disappeared into the canyon, pushing its load of silk before it.

He stopped, winded, and stared after it, rage surging up through him so that he was no longer conscious of the chill wind. "They stole the train," he muttered half aloud. "They stole the whole train." He turned back toward the deserted platform and saw people moving down the town's single street, heading for the station.

Two figures hurried ahead of the rest and reached the circle of the platform lights almost at the same instant as

113

he did. He was surprised to see that they were Tracy and Tony.

"Ran!" she said. "You're all right, Ran?"

He looked back up the spur track. "They stole the train." His voice was dull. "They stole the Silk Express." The anger was crowding up within him.

"I've got to get to the key. I've got to let Bullock know."

"It wasn't your fault," she said, and caught his arm.

"It was my fault. I was hiding in Tony's shanty when I should have been guarding the station." He pulled free and half ran toward the yellow building. He didn't see the three quiet forms lying in the shadow just outside the baggage room door. The bulge of the bay hid them from his eyes. He ran in through the waiting room and flung himself into the chair before the instrument. Not until he had pounded out half his message did he become aware that the instrument was dead.

He stared at it helplessly for a minute and then said dully, "They must have cut the wire," and came out of his chair.

Tracy was standing in the connecting doorway with Tony at her shoulder. Lonnigan almost pushed them out of the way. His one thought was to find the break in the wire and to repair it. He moved out of the station and along the platform and stopped as the lights from the bay showed him the three still figures.

For an instant he thought that all three were dead. The first one he recognized was McCable and he instinctively tried to stop Tracy, but he was too late, for she was already at his elbow.

She saw her father and gave a little deep-throated cry and brushed past Lonnigan, dropping to her knees on the rough boards to cradle McCable's head in her small arms.

Lonnigan had seen that the others were Jacoby and Dan Goodhue, but even as he bent down Goodhue groaned, stirred and sat up shakily, his eyes vacant.

Lonnigan propped him against the wall. "Where are you hit?"

Goodhue shook his head. He had no distinct recollection of exactly what had happened, and it was several minutes before his head cleared enough for him to talk.

"Halleran shot them," he said slowly and painfully.

The townspeople had come crowding across the tracks,

but still hanging back, curious, yet not ready to be identified with this.

Lonnigan turned to look at them. "Any of you a doctor?"

A short man pushed forward and knelt at Tracy's side. Lonnigan heard the man murmur, "He can't be moved. He won't last long." Lonnigan turned to Jacoby. There was no question about Jacoby. He did not need anyone to tell him that the man was dead.

Pounding on the baggage room door attracted him, and he hurriedly released the imprisoned trainmen. After that everything was confusion. He recalled nothing clearly during the next few minutes. He was helping the doctor. Someone had brought blankets from the bunkroom and they rolled McCable onto one gently and carried him inside.

"He's gut-shot," said the doctor, "clear through the middle. There isn't a chance." And then surprisingly Terry McCable opened his eyes.

His thin mouth was a little twisted from the pain in his stomach, but he managed a small smile for his daughter. "Don't cry, baby." It was only a whisper, and then he saw Lonnigan standing behind the kneeling girl and his whisper gained a little strength. "Tell Bullock," he managed. "Tell him they mean to hide the silk in an old mine and to haul it down the outlaw trail when the hunt is over." He breathed deeply and then his eyes closed. He died with the tiny smile still on his lips.

TWENTY-SEVEN

To KATE JACOBY the whole evening had been one long nightmare. Made restless by her foreknowledge of the holdup, she would much rather have accompanied Koyner to the railroad station, but the outlaw's orders had been definite.

"Stay out of sight," he warned her. "Tomorrow this town will be swarming with Pinkerton men and railroad detectives, and if anyone saw you with me you'd be in trouble. You have to stay at the hotel where you can be seen. You mustn't know anything about the holdup."

She knew that Koyner was right. She could not afford to be involved. As soon as the silk was safely hidden, Koyner and his men would head south for Mexico. From there Koyner meant to return to New Orleans where, under an assumed name, he would wait until Kate sent word that the railroad and Pinkertons had given up on the hunt. It might be six months, it might be a full year. When the time came she would get word to Koyner and he would organize the transportation of the silk down through the long weary miles to the Mexican border. There it would be transshipped to his agents in Europe.

She had to remain in the Junction to serve as Koyner's eyes, and there must be no suspicion that she had any knowledge of the holdup. She made herself conspicuous in the lobby, since she wanted to be certain that she had an alibi. Clara Bishop was behind the high desk, but aside from the landlady's colorless daughter, the lobby was empty.

Kate walked restlessly over to the big front windows and stared out across the deserted gallery at the dark, semi-empty street, then unable to remain quiet she turned and came back to the desk and stood silently watching Clara post the ledger. She was there when the first shot sounded from the station.

Clara raised her head. Her muddy blue eyes were blank with a defeated, hopeless look. "What's that?"

Kate shrugged. "You've been here long enough not to

worry about a gunshot." She tried to speak casually, but her heart was thumping so loudly that she was afraid Clara would hear it.

Clara gave her a long, studying look. "You don't like it at the Junction either." She said this slowly, as if she found the idea surprising. "Why don't you go away somewhere, Kate?"

Kate Jacoby looked at her. She had known Clara Bishop for five or six years, and yet she knew absolutely nothing about her. The girl's personality was as colorless and as unobtrusive as the faded lobby wallpaper.

"What are you talking about?"

Clara put down her snub-nosed pen. "This country's no good for a woman." She spoke in a high, nasal drawl that told plainly her midwestern origin. "Look at Maw—washed out. What's she got to live for?"

Kate had never actually thought about what Mrs. Bishop had to live for. "Well . . . I don't know . . ."

"Nothing," said Clara. "The country may be all right for men. They can go riding and drinking and helling around, shooting up the station when they have a skin full . . . What is there for a woman to do?" She sighed and picked up her pen, bending her head above the ruled page.

Kate looked at Clara for a long moment, astonished to find that behind her drab exterior Clara Bishop was as dissatisfied as she was. She started to speak, but instead walked again to the window. She was there when the train came in. She saw her father emerge from the Big Horn, trailed by Goodhue, and turn down toward the station.

She almost rushed to the door, almost called to him to stop, but she hesitated, and by the time she reached the door it was too late. Her father was halfway to the station. But she did go out to the porch, unable to remain longer inside, unmindful of the stinging wind.

She heard the two shots, sharp and clear in the windy darkness, and something warned her what had happened, for almost at once the train began to reverse and pull backward out of the yard, leaving the station platform seemingly empty.

And suddenly the street was filled with people. They had been hiding in doorways, watching events at the lower end of the street. But they moved out now and it was all that Kate could do to hold herself, to keep from joining them.

Then she saw a small group coming up the street, pushing their way through the crowd which split to let them pass. She stood gripping the rail until they moved close enough to see that Goodhue walked ahead, followed by four men who carried something in a blanket stretched between them.

Goodhue reached the foot of the wide steps and raised his eyes and saw her standing in the shadows.

"I'm sorry, Kate." His voice was not quite steady, and it was the first time that he had ever called her Kate. "I've got bad news."

She guessed what it was and drew one long, sharp breath. "Father . . . ?"

"He's dead," said Goodhue and came up the steps to put a steadying arm about her shoulders. "Jocko Halleran shot him." He added, almost as an afterthought, "He shot McCable too."

Kate had difficulty controlling a desire to laugh and wondered if she were hysterical. For some reason she couldn't think of her father. She knew that she should grieve, but somehow she could not focus her attention on her father. All she could think of was Koyner and the silk train. Koyner was safe. The silk train was theirs.

TWENTY-EIGHT

ON HER KNEES beside her father's body, Tracy McCable tried to think. It had all come so suddenly that she made no effort to fight the shock of her grief. Yet she was not a person who cried easily, and she did not cry now. She felt Lonnigan's hands under her elbows, felt him lift her to her feet and heard his comforting murmur without understanding the words.

Suddenly she was filled with a sense of loneliness, of loss. Whatever his other weaknesses, her father had always been there when she wanted him, and in the six years since her mother's death they had wandered from one end of the country to the other.

She knew very little about him. He had seldom spoken of his life in the old country, or of possible relatives there. As far as she knew she was alone in the world. Finally she became conscious that Lonnigan was still steadying her and she straightened, pulling free.

"I'm all right. Let me go." She turned to the doctor who was busy patching up Pat Burke's split skull and said in a low voice, "Do me a favor, Doc. Have Terry taken up to Benson's. Tell Benson a plain box. Terry was a plain man and he wouldn't rest easy in a fancy coffin."

The doctor nodded and turned back to Burke. The special's engineer was in bad shape. Halleran's gun barrel had broken his head in half a dozen places. He groaned, thinking not so much of himself but more of his lost train, and he looked at Lonnigan.

"You've got to get a rider off to Bullock. And then you've got to go after that train."

Lonnigan looked around the crowd and only then realized that Dan Goodhue was no longer there. For a moment he felt almost as lost as Tracy McCable did, then suddenly he knew that he, to all effects, was the railroad. It was his responsibility. Burke was incapacitated. Dan Goodhue had shown no indication of leadership, nor did the rest of the railroad employees of the Junction.

For most of his life Ran Lonnigan had left decisions

to others. As long as his Uncle Charley had lived Lonnigan had been content to bow to what he considered the older man's superior judgment. But Uncle Charley wasn't here. Bullock wasn't here . . . He took a deep breath and, turning, looked at the crowd.

"We'll take the work train," he said. "We can haul forty or fifty men. How many guns are there?"

No one answered him. They stared back, their faces blank and neutral. He turned to Swansen, the work-train engineer. Swansen had been roughed thoroughly by Koyner's men. His nose was broken and one eye was turning purple. The labor foreman stood beyond him, waiting for the doctor's services, his right arm hanging broken and useless at his side.

Lonnigan regretted the foreman; at least he was a natural fighting man. The rest of the labor crew were more than useless—ignorant, unlettered workers who had been kicked and beaten by life until they had little or no spirit left.

Swansen shrugged and moved away toward his engine, followed by his fireman who limped noticeably. Lonnigan turned back to the assembled townsmen. "Okay. I'm waiting for volunteers."

No one answered, and anger came up into Lonnigan to make his voice unsteady. "What's the matter with you?"

It was Benson who answered. The storekeeper had been almost the last person to join the crowd. "Let the railroad chase its train," he said. "We have to live in these hills with Koyner and his men."

Lonnigan centered his attack on Benson. "What's the matter with you?" he repeated. "You're afraid, but you should be more afraid. You saw Mars Jacoby shot down tonight. If they will kill Jacoby none of you are safe unless you combine and wipe them out."

They still watched him uneasily, uncertainly. Most of them were townsmen; few if any were familiar with firearms or their use. The ones on the back row turned to fade uneasily into the darkness.

Lonnigan watched them in helpless anger, but there was a worse blow to come, for Swansen tramped back along the platform, pushing his way through the press.

"That engine ain't going anywhere," he said. "They knocked out the connections. I guess no one chases after Koyner this night."

Lonnigan stared at him for a moment, then without a word he went into the station, grabbed his jacket from the peg and shrugged into it, stalking back to the platform. He shoved his way across the tracks and headed up the street.

Tracy McCable had been listening wordlessly. She suddenly jumped forward, elbowing her way after him. "Ran! Wait! You hear me, Ran Lonnigan. You wait."

Lonnigan heard her, but he was too angry to stop, and she was forced to run to catch up, grasping his arm as she came abreast. "Where do you think you are going?"

They were alone, the station with its crowd a hundred yards behind them, standing in the center of the deserted street.

"I'm going after them," he said. "What did you think I would do—let Koyner get away with it?"

"There are twenty-five of them," she said, "maybe thirty. I didn't have time to count them before Indian Pete took me up and locked me in the livery stable office."

"I don't care if there are a hundred."

"You are a silly fool," she said. "What good will it do the railroad if you get yourself killed?"

"I'm not going to get killed." Unconsciously he straightened the gun in his holster and turned again up the street, walking so rapidly that the girl was forced to dance in a little skipping step to keep up.

"You will get killed, and I don't want you to be killed. I don't think I could stand it if you get killed."

He stopped to look at her, and some of the anger was gone from his voice. "I'm not exactly a fool," he told her. "I know that one man can't recover that train, but if I can get up there in time I can see where they hide it."

"And how do you hope to get up there?"

"On a horse," he said. He was curbing his impatience with difficulty. "I'll follow the spur up to the dam site."

"No you won't," she told him. "The tracks cross three canyons, and the trestles are only ties, and you can't ride a horse across them because it would put a foot between the ties and break a leg."

"Then I'll ride around the trestles."

"You can't because the canyons are deep and the walls are steep, and it is already snowing up there and you would never make it."

"You can think of more arguments than a Philadelphia

lawyer," he said. "All right, I'll ride up the canyon and around by the trail."

"It's twenty miles," she said, "or maybe twenty-five, and probably you'll never get there before the train is unloaded, but anyhow I'll show you a short-cut."

"You?"

She nodded. "I know a path up the canyon side—I guess maybe I am about the only one who knows it—and I certainly couldn't tell you where it is so that you would find it in the dark, but I can show you."

He hesitated for a moment, and it was now Tracy McCable who took the lead, hurrying ahead to the livery stable. Lonnigan caught her at the entrance of the runway. "You saddle the horses," she flung at him across her shoulder. "I'll see what I can find in the way of guns." She walked through the office door, hanging now splintered on its hinges.

Lonnigan looked at the door. "What happened here?"

"I did," said Tracy McCable. "Indian Pete locked me in. I called and called and no one came, so I broke it down." She disappeared somewhere in the office while Lonnigan went back to saddle two horses.

TWENTY-NINE

KATE JACOBY followed the blanket bearers up the stairs
and watched them lay her father's body on the bed. They
moved out, hats removed, voices hushed as they mur-
mured their regrets.

She hardly heard them. She thought they had all gone
and was startled when she turned to find Dan Goodhue
standing just inside the door.

His small, freckled face was marred with the depth of
his feeling, and his voice was not steady. "Kate, if there's
anything I can do . . ."

She shook her head slowly.

"I'll do anything," he said, "anything. I love you, Kate."
Then he turned and fled as if terrified by his own words.

She stared after him, struck dumb for a moment by
surprise, then her mouth softened a little. Poor little man,
she thought. She had always thought of him as that little
man. He means well, but he doesn't understand—no one
can ever understand.

She turned then and looked at her father, surprised
to see how quiet and relaxed his face looked in death.
There was no trace of pain or conflict. Mars Jacoby had
died too quickly to know what had happened. It was, she
felt, the way that he would have wanted to die. He had
been too strong a man to have ever been content unless
he could be the leader. Standing there she hoped that
when her time came she could go as quickly, and then
she turned, muttering to herself that she was a fool, for
death seemed very far away.

And almost at once she forgot her father, her mind
reverting to Koyner, riding the stolen train. She stepped
back into the hall and heard confused voices below stairs.
What was happening in the lobby, in the town? What
would the citizens of the Junction do?

She felt that she had to know, but she did not want to
be seen, and then she remembered the tiny balcony outside the front window at the end of the upper hall. It was

only four feet square, built on short posts which rested for support on the slanting roof of the gallery.

Quickly she ran toward the window and slid it open to step out into the chilly darkness, shutting it behind her. Here she stood unnoticed, having a bird's-eye view of the main street and down its full length to the station beyond the tracks.

The lower end of the street was filled with people, crowding forward so that they blocked her view, and her lips curled a little as she thought that they were like so many leaderless sheep. There was no danger in them. Koyner had studied them and judged them correctly, and then she saw Ran Lonnigan cross the tracks and Tracy McCable rush after him. She saw them pause and argue, and then saw them move on and enter the livery stable. Even before they appeared on their rented horses and turned up the canyon she guessed what they were about and her hands gripped the porch railing until her nails hurt. This was something which neither she nor Koyner had foreseen. The very fact that Lonnigan was alive was disquieting, for she had known without being told directly that the plans had called for his death during the station attack.

But he was alive, spurring up the street after Tracy McCable as the younger girl turned her horse into the upper road and disappeared into the mouth of the canyon.

They were going after Koyner and his men. That much was obvious, for certainty there was no other reason for them to ride into the high hills, especially in the teeth of the approaching storm.

But what they could hope to accomplish escaped her for the moment, although she did not think that the two of them hoped to recapture the silk train. And then she dismissed the conjecture and reasoned that they merely meant to spy on Koyner as his men unloaded the stolen goods and hauled it across the divide to the abandoned mine.

Her mind measured distance against time. Would they reach the bridge site before the last of the silk had been hauled to safety? They might, for undoubtedly the tracks of the wagons would show in the falling snow, and Koyner would not even know that they had been there. He would send the emptied train back to the Junction and then begin his long ride south, believing that the whole operation had been a complete success.

124

Tomorrow or the next day Lonnigan would lead the railroad detectives to the mine. They would pull out the silk, reload it on the train and send it on its way to the eastern market. And all their work, their planning, would come to naught.

The thought almost brought tears to her eyes. But Kate Jacoby was never one to waste time on tears. She turned and reopened the window to step through to the hall. Never before had she changed clothes so rapidly. She dressed, and she lifted her small pearl-handled revolver from the dresser drawer and slipped it into her pocket, then she quickly went downstairs.

There were half a dozen people in the lobby, clustered around the desk, talking excitedly of Jacoby's death and of the holdup. Their talk ceased as she came down the stairs and their eyes followed her as she ignored them and, crossing the room quickly, went out into the night.

The street outside was filling up as people strayed back from the station. She saw Goodhue on the far sidewalk before the Big Horn and ignored him and moved quickly to the livery stable.

It was too bad that half a hundred people should see her ride out of town. The Pinkertons would certainly question her about the ride tomorrow, but it could not be helped. She ran into the stable building and, going to the rear stall, hastily saddled her own horse. Then she rode out, turned up the street and headed for the canyon at a gallop.

THIRTY

LONNIGAN had a feeling of unreality as he followed Tracy McCable up the twisting canyon. The girl was less than a dozen feet ahead of him but it was hard to see her, for the cloud bank which had been hovering over the peaks to the north had moved over, driven by the gusty wind, until it had blotted out the stars.

The air was colder here and they were riding directly into the wind and the smell of snow was sharp and clear. They held their steady gait against the rising grade for two full miles before the girl turned sidewise from the main trail and followed a crooked path which Lonnigan could barely see through the stunted, wind-twisted timber.

He sensed, rather than saw, that the ground was steepening abruptly and guessed that they were following a hogback which ran into the canyon wall at an oblique angle.

It was, he thought, a crazy thing to ride thus in the darkness over an unknown trail toward a canyon wall which rose ahead endlessly until it seemed to reach the darkness of the threatening sky. The horse shared its rider's uncertainty, for it had slowed to a walk, picking its way forward as if it expected that each step would be its last.

Lonnigan had a momentary doubt, wondering if Tracy was purposely leading him into a blind pocket in an effort to keep him from tackling Koyner's men. It was, he supposed, exactly what she might do if she believed that by the action she could keep him safe.

But even as he opened his mouth to call to her the trees thinned and they came up to the wall at a point where a narrow stream dashed down from above in its hurry to join the main river below them.

Through the years this plunging riverlet had cut a side canyon of its own and into this Tracy urged her reluctant horse, bearing upward with the sure confidence of past experience, never once looking back.

Lonnigan rode close behind, his mount surging and

stumbling on the slippery stones, at times almost going to its knees. So they climbed for what he judged must have been at least three hundred feet, and suddenly the tiny canyon widened into a basin which was, he saw, about the size of the Junction station.

Here Tracy dismounted, small and slender as she moved to her horse's head and comforted his blowing protest.

Lonnigan swung down, putting a reassuring hand on his own mount's trembling flanks. "Easy, boy. Easy." He turned to look at Tracy. Her face was not distinct, merely a tiny whiteness between the wings of her turned-up coat collar. "Some climb." He tried to make his tone casual.

"It's worse above." They were protected in this pocket from the full sweep of the wind, and she spoke matter-of-factly in a normal tone. "There's a ledge—not much wider than a chair. Once we're across that face the rest is fairly easy. But we'll have to lead the horses across the ledge."

He felt a small stab of dismay. "How in the world did you ever find this trail?"

"I like to climb," said Tracy McCable. "Climbing does something for me. It's kind of like having yourself opened up and made free."

Lonnigan was silent for a moment before he asked, "It's easier to climb than it is to go down. How did you ever manage to get a horse to descend that trail?"

"I never brought a horse up here before. I climbed on foot."

He stared at her through the masking darkness, wishing suddenly that he could see her small, reassuring face. "Tracy," he said, "you're quite a guy."

"Ha," she said. "You were an unconscionable time in finding that out." She did not wait for his answer but turned away, leading her horse toward the shelf.

Lonnigan followed. Once out of the shelter of the pocket they encountered the full force of the blasting wind. He would much rather have gone ahead, but there was no room for him to get around Tracy's mount and it was certainly not the place for an argument.

And Tracy would argue, no matter in what position she found herself. That much he had learned about her.

The uneven shelf slanted up gently as it cut across the bare rock of the face. They felt their way, rather than saw, exactly where they were going. He leaned inward against the wall, keeping the reins tight so that his horse

127

could not falter. Actually, he trusted the animal's instinct better than his own sight.

Ahead, he heard Tracy murmuring encouragement to her own mount. He could not hear her words against the violence of the wind, but the even tone of her voice was in itself reassuring.

Below them he could hear the wind beating through the scrub foliage and he had to fight down the impulse to hurry, to push onward, to be clear of the ledge.

He had no idea how far below him lay the canyon floor. It was too dark even to see the moving tops of the trees, and then abruptly they came off the ledge and found themselves in the center of another draw which another stream had cut down through the rim of the canyon wall.

He could hear the tumultuous motion of the water above the wind, although he could not see the stream itself, for below them the water shot off into space in a hollow thunder which carried it three or four hundred feet to the canyon floor below.

Tracy was pressed close to his side, one small hand on his arm, her voice almost against his ear, trying to make herself heard against the roar.

"From here up it's a cinch," she said. "There's a deer path follows the stream. We can ride."

He stooped and lifted her into her saddle, and for a moment her arm was about his neck; then she wheeled and climbed from his sight. By the time he had reached his own saddle the darkness had swallowed her. And then it began to snow.

Lonnigan knew the quick spring blizzards of the mountains and he respected them, but he did not fear them. He had spent more than one night beating his way across a high mountain park with nothing to guide him but the direction of the howling wind, but the snow made the climbing hazardous, and the higher they reached upward the worse it became.

Their horses slipped and stumbled until finally Lonnigan dismounted, leading the animal until they topped out of the canyon a good fifteen hundred feet above the hogback where they had started their ascent.

And as they emerged the full impact of the wind caught them in its sweep and threatened to hurl them back down the long trail they had climbed so laboriously.

On top it had been snowing steadily for three hours

128

and the high table land which stretched away, broken and furrowed by canyons and washes until it reached the right peaks of the divide, was already blanketed by a good foot of the clinging stuff.

The fall was heavy, but the whipping wind doubled and tripled the stinging curtain as it whirled up snow which had already fallen and bore it along to pile in man-high drifts against the rough outcroppings of the barren rock.

It was blinding, breath-taking, and yet curiously enough it was easier to see here than it had been during their climb up the canyon wall, for the white snow on the ground brought a weird luminous quality to the world, a kind of dull cold light so that objects and rock upthrusts were visible faintly at twenty to thirty feet.

Lonnigan was still on foot and he pressed up close to Tracy's horse. "How far from here to the bridge site?"

Tracy's words as she answered were snatched from her chilled lips by the wind and borne so rapidly away that Lonnigan barely heard. "Four miles. We saved fifteen coming up the canyon wall."

He nodded, not trying unnecessary words, and grabbed her bridle to turn her horse half around. "I'll find it. You head back for the trail now."

"No."

He had a better idea. "You can get down into the canyon by foot. Leave your horse with me and go back. Get out of this snow."

"No." She pulled the bridle from his numb fingers and swung her horse around, pushing the unwilling animal against the wind.

He mounted with a muttered curse and went after her, having to drive his spurs cruelly into the animal's heavy flanks until he pulled abreast and, reaching out, he caught her rein.

"Listen to me," he said. "This is serious. This storm is going to get worse. Get back down the canyon. You can walk to town. Send another rider down the line to Clear Water. Have him tell Bullock where I am."

"No."

He had the sudden impulse to strike her. She was so damn hard-headed stubborn. "Tracy, listen to me. You may know a lot more big words than I do, but I know these mountains and these storms. I can get through myself, because I know how, but I'm not sure I can take care of you."

A flash of her old independence showed. "And who wants any care, Ran Lonnigan?" She wrenched the rein free and swung the unwilling horse around. Lonnigan had little choice but to follow.

THIRTY-ONE

RIDING THE CAB of the stolen Express James Koyner experienced a curious let-down. For months he had planned this holdup, dreamed this holdup, executed each and every step meticulously in his mind, and now it was an accomplished fact. From now on there would be long months of waiting while the railroad detectives searched fruitlessly for the hidden loot. Then he would come back and transfer the silk south.

Everything had gone fairly smoothly. He had expected to trap the night operator inside the station and either kill him or make him prisoner in the baggage room. He wondered half idly how Lonnigan had escaped from the station and decided that he did not care.

And he had not anticipated opposition from Mars Jacoby. That had come as a complete surprise, but the way it had worked out was probably much better. He felt no sorrow for Jacoby's death, and he had known from the first that McCable would have to die, although he had planned to kill him in the hills and not at the station.

McCable was much too unstable a character to have taken with them on the flight south. The lunchroom man when sober always had developed a distressing sense of guilt at his own actions.

No, nothing about the holdup bothered Koyner, not even the fear of what her father's death might do to Kate, but it had been too easy. He was a man who thrived on competition. He did not crave violence as Jocko Halleran did, but he needed the stimulation of a contest, a battle of wits, and he wished that there were some way he might have remained in town to watch the baffled railroad men in their search for the stolen silk.

He peered out of the window of the reversing train as it backed up the cutoff. Long before they reached the bridge site they had gained enough altitude so that they had run into the storm.

The snow would make everything perfect. It was almost as if the elements had conspired with him in his efforts to leave no trail that could be followed. The higher they climbed the heavier became the fall, and he had a momentary fear before they reached the bridge site that it might grow deep enough to bog down the ore wagons which his men had stolen for their transport.

They pulled finally onto the siding, so close to the skeleton cribbing of the new bridge that he could see the raised arms, despite the drifting snow, and the train had hardly stopped moving before the outlaws were off and already at work. They worked with clocklike precision. Each man had his place and knew his assignment thoroughly. It was a tribute to Koyner's genius for organization that there was utterly no confusion. One car after another was broken into and the bales hauled out and loaded into the waiting ore wagons. Had there been enough wagons to transport the whole trainload at one time the operation would have been virtually completed before Lonnigan and Tracy ever saw the white glare of the locomotive's headlamp shining at them through the storm.

As it was, the drifting snow was so thick that they almost rode their horses across the track before they became aware of how far they had come and were forced to turn back to seek the shelter of a strip of timber which paralleled the right-of-way.

Fortunately Koyner had not placed any guards, not feeling the need of them and wanting every man available to help handle the heavy bales.

Neither Lonnigan nor Tracy knew this. Quickly they slipped back into the half-shelter of the timber and, dismounting, led their horses along cautiously until they reached the work road which led from the unloading spur down to the bridge site.

This road cut down the canyon side in long, looping curves, crossed on a coffer dam and climbed the far slope to disappear onto the high plateau beyond.

Crouched, half blinded, but still protected from sight by the flying snow, they watched the road as one loaded ore cart after another made the treacherous descent, crossed the stream and climbed from their sight across the canyon.

Lonnigan leaned so close to Tracy that his lips brushed the edge of her small ear. "Wonder where they got the teams and wagons?"

"From Jacoby's mines."

"And I suppose they'll hide the silk in one of his properties?"

"Or in one of the abandoned tunnels over west. There must be hundreds of them."

"All of that." He stood up, hoping to see more clearly against the white night. "They haven't got enough wagons to move the whole load at once; they'll be here a good part of the night. I've got to get across the canyon. You'd better go back."

"I don't know whether I could find my way."

He turned to look at her, and suddenly he realized how small and half frozen she was. "I've got to get you out of here."

"Where?"

He didn't know.

"I'll come with you," she said. "I'd rather be with you than alone."

He reached out, putting an arm around her slight shoulders and pulling her tight against him for a moment. "You've got a lot of grit, Tracy."

"Have I . . . ?" She sounded pleased, although the small triangle of her face looked blue with cold.

"I'd better try to get you back to town."

"And not find out where they are hiding the silk? Don't be silly." She turned and swung herself stiffly up into her saddle. "I'm not cold. Come on."

He followed her, filled with misgivings. Instead of abating as he had hoped, the storm seemed to be increasing in fury, the snow in spots was so deep that their horses went through it in plunging motions. At others the wind had swept the rough ground almost bare.

They cut up-canyon a hundred yards above the work road and dropped over the edge, slipping and sliding as they worked their way to the canyon bottom. Here the stream ran placidly between long gravel bars. They crossed without difficulty, but they could not scale the far bank and were forced to double back downstream to the coffer dam. It was warmer in the canyon bottom. The wind was only a roar high above their heads and the mantle of snow was not so heavy. They waited until a gap opened in the moving wagons and then, taking the chance that they would not be observed, turned their horses into the beaten path of the road and followed it toward the canyon rim above.

133

THIRTY-TWO

KATE JACOBY rode harder than she had ever ridden in her life. But she was mountain-bred and she had spent almost as much time on horseback as she had in walking. She rode easily, pushing her mount on the fairly level stretches and allowing it to walk up the steeper grades. The last thing she wanted to do on this night was to kill her horse.

And the horse was a good one. She had broken him herself and no one else had ever been on his back, but she knew that it would take all his endurance if she reached the bridge site in time to warn Koyner.

She really expected to catch Lonnigan and the younger girl on the trail, and she loosened the revolver in readiness, but, although she rode faster than anyone had ever climbed the canyon before, she still had no sight of them.

Before she had traveled five miles the snow began swirling about her, borne on the teeth of the driving downdraft. She bent her head, in a dim hope of finding tracks which Lonnigan might have made, but saw none.

The horse, wiser than she, fought to twist away from the storm, but she held it grimly to the trail, curbing it viciously with the wicked Spanish bit, driving forward, forcing it to the limit of its strength.

Whatever happened, Koyner and his men must be warned in time to cut off Lonnigan. If they were free, if they saw where the silk was hidden, all their plans would come to naught.

Time seemed endless as she rode through the storm. Only her driving spirit forced her ahead. Her hands and feet were numb and she was certain that her cheeks were frozen beneath the scarf which she had pulled up almost to her eyes.

She had no way of telling exactly how long the ride took. She reached the canyon top and curved back along the rim toward the distant bridge site, angered by the knowledge that only a scant two thousand feet below her was the road up which she had traveled from the Junction.

If there had only been a path, a short cut up the canyon wall, she could have saved at least an hour, perhaps more, but she finally broke through the thin timber and saw the train, blanketed by the falling snow, its car doors standing open while the outlaws swarmed about it.

One of them saw her as she rode up beside the engine and Koyner turned quickly, running forward through the snow which was now nearly two feet on the level, drawing his gun as he came, not knowing who it was.

They had almost finished the unloading; another half-hour while the creaking carts made their slow, tortuous trip and the substitute engineer would move the express back to the Junction yards, leaving the looted train to be found abandoned when the railroad officials finally broke through from the Division Point.

For a minute as he ran forward Koyner did not recognize the snow-covered figure which stood beside the blowing horse, then he saw that it was Kate, and his voice was harsh with quick anger as he plowed to a stop at her side.

"I thought I told you not to stir from the hotel."

Koyner had never used that tone to Kate Jacoby before. In fact, no man had, with the possible exception of her father, and had she been less tired, less cold, less miserable, her anger would have come up to match his, but she was past anger, almost past caring.

"It's Lonnigan," she gasped. "He and the McCable girl are somewhere in the hills. I followed them up the canyon, but I couldn't catch them."

Koyner and the girl were no longer alone. The outlaws, their faces beef-red from the wind, ice and snow clinging to their whiskers, crowded around them, a tight circle which almost made a windbreak for the girl.

Chad Crawford came through the circle, his scarred face masked by the protecting muffler which he wore, and caught the girl's shoulder, saying in quick, worried words,

"Kate, in the name of land, what are you doing here?"

The girl ignored him. Koyner disregarded him, saying tensely, "You think they were coming here?"

"Where else would they come in the face of this blizzard?"

He considered for a moment. Crawford looked from one to the other, his temper made raw by the weather and his emotions. He was not a man whose mind functioned rapidly and it had taken very little effort on the part of either Kate or Koyner to deceive him, but he realized now that the girl had not ridden into the hills because of him, that her whole attention and whole interest was centered on the outlaw leader, and bitter resentment rose up through him like a slow-burning fuse.

And the fact that Koyner paid him not the slightest attention quickened the anger, but Koyner's mind was too engrossed with the new problem to be even conscious of Crawford.

He said, thoughtfully, "And they were ahead of you?"

She nodded. "Unless they lost their way in the storm."

Koyner turned his head. "Pete!"

The half-breed moved silently out of the circle of men to his side.

Koyner's voice was crisp. "You heard. Lonnigan is somewhere in these hills. He may be watching us now. With this damn snow a man could stand a dozen feet away and you wouldn't know whether he was enemy or friend. Find him."

The half-breed nodded and moved away. He circled the train, like a hound that has lost the scent and hopes to pick it up again. He widened his circle and they lost him as he disappeared into the scrub timber.

Koyner turned and caught the girl's arm. "There's a stove in the caboose, and coffee there. Come on. Jake, take care of her horse." He started to move with her along the train, but Chad Crawford shifted to block their way.

"I'll take care of her, Koyner. She's my woman. She's given me her word."

Through Kate's numbness rose a sharp impatience. All she wanted at the moment was a fire and hot coffee to warm her icy body. Had she not been so uncomfortable she would yet have played up to Crawford's vanity, since it was easier to control men with sugared words than by blows. But at this time she was past all pretense, past all caring. Crawford had served his purpose. They had needed someone who understood the telegraph code, who could decipher for them the railroad orders which flashed over the wire, and she had recruited Crawford with promises, letting him believe that it was he she loved, that it was he she intended to marry.

"Don't be a fool," she said, and tried to step by him.

Chad Crawford's face got a drawn look as if the life

136

had been washed out of him. He stood for a moment, his arms hanging at his sides, and then he stepped wordlessly out of the way, only to change his mind, to swing back as his slow mind grasped the fact that he had been tricked. He reached out for the girl's arm, but Koyner struck him aside.

Then Crawford turned on Koyner, making an animal noise deep in his throat as he tried to draw his gun. He never got it fully clear of the holster, for Jocko Halleran shot him where he stood, shot him twice and then holstered his gun almost before Crawford had toppled forward into the snow.

Koyner did not even waste a glance at the fallen man, nor did he trouble to throw a glance of thanks at the grinning Halleran. He turned instead, steering Kate along the train to the caboose at the rear, boosting her up the iron steps and into the overheated room. There he was pouring the second cup of scalding coffee into her when Indian Pete swung up to the snowy platform and slid open the door.

"Tracks," he said, before Koyner could ask the question. "Two horses. They stand and watch us from the timber, then they slide down the canyon and go up road after wagons."

"How long ago?" Koyner prompted.

"Can't tell. Wind blow snow, fill tracks fast. Maybe hour, maybe half."

Koyner frowned thoughtfully. Jocko Halleran had come up the steps behind the Indian. Koyner made his decision. "Get the rest of the silk out of these cars fast. Have Boyce run the train down to the Junction. You ride with him, Pete. Take Sullivan and Barney with you. Get horses and ride back up the canyon trail. Watch as you come up. Don't let Lonnigan and the girl get past you. Understand?"

The breed nodded. Koyner looked speculatively at Halleran. "Take three men and see if you can follow Lonnigan's tracks. I'll pay a thousand dollars gold to the man who kills that damned railroad agent. The rest of us will load the silk and follow. We'll meet at Shaw's Flats. If we don't find them tonight we'll have to stay here until we do."

THIRTY-THREE

THE OLD CLAFLIN MINE was made to order as a hiding place for the stolen silk. It had been worked out two years before by three brothers who had come north from Cripple Creek during the short rush which had populated this section of the mountains with three thousand miners.

The miners were gone; the ore had proved highly complex and, while it existed in workable quantities, the milling and smelter penalties and the hauling costs had eaten away any profits. The whole district was honeycombed with abandoned properties; the only mines which were still operating were the three which Mars Jacoby worked halfheartedly.

Every canyon within a radius of five miles had its old headframe, its twisted shaft house and its decaying mill. There was little to choose between them, but after careful study Koyner had selected the Claflin. It was a dry mine. There was no water in its slanting shaft and only a little at the sump level. Then, the underground workings were fairly extensive and fairly deep. The single-compartment shaft slanted into the hill for a good seven hundred feet and the drifts and cross cuts were nearly five miles in length. There was no danger of cavage, since the rock stood well without timbering, and the mine was not too far from the bridge site and yet not so close that the railroad men would consider it the obvious hiding place.

All these things had weighed with Koyner when he made his selection and the actual spot where the silk would rest was as nearly perfect as possible. It was a stoped-out room on the three-hundred-foot level. The room had been dug along the pitching vein, connected with the tunnel by a small ore chute. It would be simple to store the stolen goods, and then blow down the wall so that the chute would be completely choked with shattered rock. Since during the mine's operation, all county rock had been stored underground in the worked-out rooms, there would be nothing to attract the railroad investigators to that particular spot, or even that particular mine.

They could spend years searching the old workings and never locate the silk which had been looted from the Express. It would be worse than hunting a needle in a haystack, or a chip of marble in a quarry, but if a man knew where the silk was hidden it would be only a matter of hours to clear out the debris and recover the hidden bales.

Neither Ran Lonnigan nor Tracy McCable had any idea where they were heading as they pushed their horses up the looping grade above the bridge site.

Ahead and behind they could hear the squeaking grind of the ungreased ore carts above the howl of the wind. They had little fear of discovery since the air was clogged with driving snow, and even if they were seen by one of the wagon drivers Lonnigan felt sure that the man would mistake them for members of the outlaw band.

Even after they topped out of the canyon, they still rode on in the wheel tracks. It was so much easier riding the path furrowed by the wagons than it was to attempt to cut across the unbroken country. The drifts were five to six feet deep and on the level the snow lay a good twenty inches thick. The tired horses were only too glad to progress at a slow walk which would not overtake the lumbering wagons.

And then they began to meet wagons coming back, empty, returning for another load. The first almost caught them unawares coming suddenly out of the snowy blanket which drove like a stinging curtain against their faces. Lonnigan saw the dark shape emerge just in time and pushed his mount sidewise, turning the girl's horse with him.

The cart lumbered past, not missing them by a dozen feet. It was followed by a second, a third, and then a fourth.

Afterwards there was a break and they returned to the trail, pushing ahead until the trail twisted into the side canyon on the west slope, on which perched the gaunt outline of the Claflin headframe.

As soon as he saw it, showing intermittently through the gusts of white flakes, Lonnigan knew where he was. As a boy he had ridden this whole section of the country, and many a piece of metal had been salvaged by the small ranchero from these abandoned workings.

At once he reined off to the right, leaving the cart tracks which turned and wound upward over the old dump. He pushed straight up the canyon floor, fighting the drifts until he was beyond the swell of the dump, then turned and climbed the slope so that the old mill, sagging in graduated steps, was between him and the lighted shaft house.

The yellow light from the lanterns showed one cart pulled up before the door, a second standing behind it, waiting to be unloaded, a third slowly climbing the hill.

Lonnigan pushed his horse into the lee made by the creaking mill building and swung down, turning as Tracy rode to his side. He reached up stiffly and lifted her from the saddle and motioned to her to stamp her legs and move her arms. They were both chilled to the bone, stiffened until it was painful to make a motion of any kind, but he kept her at it while the three carts were unloaded, watching the progress through the wide cracks between the weathered boards.

The men above him were working rapidly, wrestling the heavy bales out of sight almost as soon as they slid down from the carts, and Lonnigan found himself marveling at the hardships that the outlaws would undergo to steal. Not one of the men above would have considered working one half as hard for honest wages, and it was something which Lonnigan found hard to understand.

The girl's motions had restored a part of her circulation and she moved up to his side to peer through the next crack in the sagging wall, her voice trembling a little with excitement and cold. "We've found it," she whispered. "We've found where the silk is hidden. Now, can we go?"

"In a couple of minutes," he said. "I want to have a look in the mine first."

"Look in the mine?" she gripped his arm with one gloved hand. "You're crazier than I thought. How can you get into the mine with the outlaws in the shaft house, and what good is it going to do you?"

"I've got to." He was trying to be patient. "There are miles of old workings. We could search for days and then might not find where they hid the silk. It won't take long."

"You'll get killed," she wailed.

Lonnigan did not even bother to answer. He turned and cut around the corner of the old building. Behind him he heard Tracy call his name, but the sound came very faintly, caught as it was and carried away by the wind.

Above him the last wagon was empty and turned back down the dump, headed again for the stolen train. He had no way of knowing how quickly the next cart would arrive and if he meant to enter the mine he must do it now.

He came up to the side of the shaft house, peering through the cracks at the room inside. A lantern hung suspended on an old nail and gave him a clear view of the place. The square room was empty, the opening of the slanted shaft gaping dark and deserted in the rear wall. He circled the building and came in through the front door, drawing his gun as he entered. Nothing stirred in the shaft beyond and he crossed to its opening, peering down the thirty degree haulage tunnel.

Far below him in the darkness he could see a lantern bobbing as its carrier descended the slatted steps which ran down the side of the tunnel along the tracks of the ore car. Lonnigan moved forward, following.

The Claflins had been competent engineers and the mine was well organized. The tunnel ran down straight into the hill and followed roughly the pitch of the vein. From it, at fifty foot levels, laterals ran out into the ore body which had been stoped down through chutes to be loaded into the car which was hauled to the surface by the donkey engine and dumped down the incline into the mill below.

After the coldness of the outer air the tunnel felt warm and close and dust-filled, and Lonnigan loosened his jacket as he moved downward, knowing that he would need its protection even more when he again stepped into the storm.

He was passing the two-hundred-foot level when he saw the lantern ahead disappear and he stopped, trying to recall whether the main tunnel made a bend there. He could not remember and he remained motionless in the half-suffocating darkness, waiting until the echo of distant voices came up to him and he guessed that his guide had turned off into one of the laterals, then he moved onward, balancing his heavy gun in his hand, careful that his feet dislodged no loose rock to give away his presence to the mine guards.

At the two-hundred-and-fifty-foot level he paused again, for below him light sifted faintly from a side lateral and

141

he thought for the moment that the men were returning. But nothing happened, and taking a tighter grip on the gun he continued his descent until he reached the entrance of the drift and could peer along it.

The lantern had been placed on the tunnel floor beside a pile of silk bales which almost filled the lateral. One man was in sight, lifting the bales up through an ore chute into a stope above.

Lonnigan watched while one bale after another was handed up to the unseen man above, then he turned. The wise thing was to get out of the tunnel as quickly as possible. He had learned what he had come to the mine to find out. And he could lead the railroad detectives to the silk's hiding place without the slightest trouble.

But his natural stubbornness held him there, hesitating, for an idea had crossed his mind. He could probably capture the two men, for from the sound of the voices he had gathered that there was but a single outlaw in the stope above. He could take them and tie them up, and wait until the other wagons arrived, capturing each driver in turn as he pulled up to the shaft house.

But what would happen when the wagons remained unloaded, when they failed to return to the bridge site? Koyner and his men would come whooping to find out what had happened. It would be stupid, a useless matter of pride and it would let Koyner know that the hiding place had been discovered. The sensible thing to do would be to leave as rapidly as possible, to get Tracy and hunt shelter for the girl. Time enough to recapture the silk when Bullock arrived from the Division Point with help. He started to climb, finding it much harder than it had been to descend.

THIRTY-FOUR

LEFT TO HERSELF in the lee of the old mill building Tracy McCable continued to swing her arms and stomp her feet. She was between the horses, and their bodies offered her even more protection than came from the sagging wall, but she was still chilled. She felt as if she would never be thoroughly warm again in her life.

Time dragged out slowly. It seemed to her that Lonnigan must have been gone for hours. Her mind began to imagine everything which might have happened to him underground and for the first time since her father's sudden death she tried to look at her own future.

What if Lonnigan was captured? What if he were already dead, surprised by one of the mine guards. She realized that unconsciously she had linked her future with his. She considered this thoughtfully, objectively, as if she were no part of the picture herself. She was so engrossed with the thought that she did not see Jocko Halleran and his two men.

Halleran had followed along the wagon road on Koyner's orders until he came to the place where the wheel tracks turned off to climb the shoulder of the old dump. He stopped there, seeing the marks of their horses where Lonnigan and Tracy had ridden on up the side canyon. The wind had already drifted the tracks nearly half full but they were still plain enough for Halleran to tell that there had been two riders. He turned, motioning his men forward, and followed the tracks around the upper end of the dump to where they turned again, heading for the old mill.

Through the blowing snow he had a quick glimpse of the two horses, standing hip-shot and weary in the lee of the building and his excitement quickened as he spurred forward up the hill.

Another five minutes and they would have had Tracy, but at that moment Lonnigan stepped from the door of the shaft house. His quick eye caught the three black

143

shadows and he raised the gun he had been carrying in his hand and fired without even stopping to think.

He missed and fired again, and missed again, but Halleran, surprised by this attack from an unexpected direction, pulled up, slanting quickly off to the right, his two men spurring after him.

The shots waked Tracy McCable out of her half-dream. She spun around, seeing the three riders veering away and the next minute was in her own saddle, leading Lonnigan's horse around the corner of the mill at a slipping trot. Lonnigan ran forward to meet her, the snow making him clumsy as he snatched for his reins, but his horse was too weary to shy away. He got them on the second grab and lifted himself into the saddle.

For the moment the mill building was between them and Halleran's men and he swung his horse upward, using the structure for a shield for as long as possible. The ground around the shaft house was fairly level and Lonnigan checked his horse to look back. The mine opening was about halfway up the canyon's side and there was no hope that they could cut down toward the mouth without coming under the direct fire of Halleran and his followers.

Even as he checked the horse a rifle spoke from below and a bullet whacked its way into the headframe high above his head. He looked up the canyon, seeing that it pinched out into a box in which they would be trapped. The only escape then lay up the face behind the mine which steepened sharply before it reached the rim.

Lonnigan hesitated for a second only, then put his horse at the rising ground at the side of the shaft house. The going stiffened almost at once and he felt the tired animal quiver under him as it fought for some kind of footing in the loose snow.

Behind him he heard Tracy's voice, steady and unafraid, urging her mount upward as the rifle spoke again, kicking up a small geyser almost under the front legs of Lonnigan's horse.

Ran glanced back. Halleran and his companions were urging their horses up the first breasting of the dump, yelling as they climbed, but Lonnigan did not waste time in drawing his gun or in shooting. His one idea was to reach the rim far above their heads. It was, he felt, their sole chance of safety.

Tracy McCable realized this also. She knew that death

144

was all they could expect at the hands of Koyner's men and she pushed her horse upward, helping all she could as it lunged against the deep snow.

Even the wind seemed to be against them for it chose this minute to drop to a fitful breeze which hardly stirred the white flakes and for the first time in two hours they could see for better than two hundred feet.

Against the white canyon wall their black outline was distinct, a seemingly easy target for Halleran's ready gun. The only thing that saved them was Halleran's impatience. He drove forward, shooting as he rode, and his shots went wide because of the plunges of his horse.

But Halleran was not a man to keep making a mistake. Realizing what was happening, and that the fugitives were nearing the canyon rim, he reined in and, stepping from the saddle, steadied his rifle for four rapid shots.

The shots were low, spoiled by the angle at which he was forced to shoot, but on his fifth he took more time, and Tracy's horse staggered, tried to right itself and then rolled, throwing the girl to the ground.

Lonnigan was out of his own saddle as soon as he heard her cry. He drew his revolver and, using his other elbow to steady his shaking hand, fired deliberately until his hammer clicked on an empty cartridge. His shots fell short, but he had the pleasure of seeing Halleran scramble hurriedly back into his saddle, to see the outlaw pull away to one side.

Then he knelt quickly at Tracy's side. The girl was not hurt, but she was almost buried in the loose snow and had to fight her way out.

"Take my horse." Lonnigan shoved the reins into her hand, but when he tried to raise her into the saddle she pulled away, instead climbing toward the rim, leading the animal after her.

Lonnigan was too busy reloading his gun to pay much attention. The outlaws had straightened out their horses and were coming up again. Coolly he stood there and emptied his gun, and saw the man on Halleran's left throw up his hands and pitch screaming from the saddle.

Two rifle bullets struck so close to Lonnigan's feet that they kicked snow all over him as he again reloaded. Then he heard Tracy's cry and the sound of the gun which she had borrowed from the livery office.

"Up here! Up here. I'll cover you." She was firing deliberately and steadily and her bullets made the two outlaws cut sidewise in an effort to seek shelter behind the old mill.

Lonnigan scrambled up to the girl's side. "We've got to get out of here. That rifle will murder us."

"Look." Tracy was pointing down the hill to where the two men from the mine had raced out to greet Halleran.

Lonnigan pivoted and drove them to cover with five well-placed shots, then saw a rider drive his horse from behind the mill and race away downhill and guessed that Halleran was sending a message back to Koyner, asking help. Lonnigan threw his last shot after him, knowing that it would be short, and once again slipped new shells into his gun.

"Come on," he said, "before they bring the whole crowd back." He lifted her to the horse and this time she did not protest as he led the way up over the rim.

"Shouldn't we circle?"

Lonnigan stopped to get his bearings. The wind was freshening again, filling the air with lashing snow which made it difficult to see. "Best way," he decided, "is over the top and down into Falling Leaf."

The girl's voice sounded faint against the violence of the storm. "Think we'll make it?"

"Certainly," said Lonnigan, and wished that he was as sure as he tried to make her believe. It was a good thirty miles to Falling Leaf directly over the peaks of the divide, but they could not go back. Koyner was no fool. Koyner would see that their road back to the Junction was cut off.

THIRTY-FIVE

WHEN SHE WAS TWELVE Kate Jacoby's father had taken her on a lion hunt, and she could still recall the mounting thrill she had felt as the yapping dogs finally had cornered the big cat.

She rode now at Koyner's side, not at all certain that she was enjoying her first manhunt, but she could not bring herself to stay with the train which they were taking back to the Junction yards. She could have ridden down at ease in the warm caboose, but she realized that if she did so she would be tortured by the uncertainty of what was happening above her in the snowy hills.

Even Koyner misunderstood her reason for riding out with them. "You're a bloodthirsty devil," he said as he pressed his horse close to her side. "I didn't realize how cold-blooded you are."

She turned to look at him, meaning to explain, and then decided that it was not worth while and rode on silent, wrapped deeply in her own thoughts. It was not that she wanted Lonnigan dead, and certainly the McCable girl was not worth worrying about. It was rather that as long as they lived they were a threat to herself and to Koyner and to all their future plans.

She regretted that they must die, but she accepted the fact that their deaths were necessary and therefore tried to put it from her mind.

The wind had dropped, and although it was still snowing heavily, it was much easier to see, far more pleasant to ride. They were following the last loaded silk wagons and had traveled halfway to the Claflin Mine when they were met by Halleran's spurring messenger.

The man pulled up, his horse blowing, little circles of white frost showing about each of its nostrils.

"We've got them treed," he yelled, "on the rim above the mine. Come on."

Koyner pulled out at once, his mounted men following, circling the slow-moving wagons. Kate hesitated for a moment, then she too circled the wagon and rode toward

147

the shaft house. When she arrived, bringing her panting animal up the swell of the dump, she found Koyner dismounted and talking to Halleran.

"They can't travel far," said Halleran. "They've only got one horse and he's probably beat out. If Lonnigan knows the country they won't circle east. That way they'd run into rimrock and they can't get off the table. They can either go over the top and come down into Falling Leaf or circle northeast and try to cut around us back to the Junction trail."

"If they do," said Koyner, "they'll meet Pete and the men who are hauling the train back to the Junction. If they try to get out that way we'll have them between us. My guess is that they'll try to go over the top . . ."

Halleran shrugged, staring at the distant peaks. "Lots of snow." He was speaking softly to himself. "And the wind is rising again. It's going to be plain hell crossing that table—plain hell. If they had two horses or if Lonnigan was alone I'd say that he had once chance in five of making it. With the girl he doesn't have any."

Kate had been sitting her horse quietly, listening. "Can't we leave them to the weather?"

Koyner turned to look at her. "No, we can't. We've got to be certain." He said to one of the mine guards, "The last wagons are on their way. When you get them unloaded send them back to Jacoby's Florence Mine. When the silk is stored, blow down the wall. Make certain the chute is well covered. We all meet at Shaw's Flats in the morning."

He looked thoughtfully at the swirling snow. "Two hours of this wind and there won't be a sign to show that we've ever been here." He walked to his horse and swung up, saying to Kate as he turned, "Wouldn't you rather stay here and meet me at Shaw's Flats?"

She shook her head, and he shrugged as he urged his horse up the canyon side. They scrambled upward, noting as they did so that the tracks made by Tracy and Lonnigan were almost obliterated, and broke over the rim to feel the staggering force of the wind sweeping across the high table land.

They could see less than fifty feet, but the tracks made by the single horse were still visible and they pressed on against the slight rise of the ground, passing around irregular rocky hillocks, some of which were miniature mountains in themselves. They rode grimly, for nearly

148

all of them had been in the saddle for most of the previous day, but they were watchful, knowing that under the shelter of the snowy curtain Lonnigan might attempt to double back toward the Junction trail.

There were twelve men and the girl. The rest of the crew were with the wagons and returning the looted train to the Junction.

After they had covered a good half-mile Koyner spread his men into a kind of skirmish line. "Keep in sight of the rider next to you," he warned, "but we'll cover as much ground as we can. Watch for tracks, for they may circle at any time."

For himself, he rode forward, following Jocko Halleran who clung to Lonnigan's trail with the tenacity of a hungry bloodhound. Two men rode behind Koyner, with Kate Jacoby partially sheltered between them.

The snow thickened. It was like a shroud, blanketing anything that was over a dozen feet away. The riders on the flanks called back and forth to one another; at times their voices were their only means of contact. And on they rode, lost in a world that seemed to contain nothing anywhere but snow.

THIRTY-SIX

To TRACY McCABLE the snow was both a blessing and a curse. She knew that but for the howling blizzard their pursuers would already have closed in. But the wind striking against her small body seemed to knife through it, deadening her senses and her perception. Looking back at Lonnigan who plodded behind her laboring horse she envied him.

Walking would bring a certain warmth, and he was not as exposed as she was on the horse's back. She fought a growing drowsiness, recognizing the danger, but still only half able to throw off the stupefying torpor which seemed to drug her senses and make it difficult for her to concentrate on anything.

The horse she rode was hardly in better shape. It blundered into drifts which came up to the saddle girth, struggling, fighting, lunging forward in exhausted efforts to keep its feet.

The circle of vision was restricted and around them was nothingness, no sound save the rush of the wind. Nothing existed for her save the straining horse and Lonnigan following somehow through the path that the horse's passage made.

She swayed in the saddle, and somehow Lonnigan saw her, and somehow he was at her side, reaching up to steady her. She did not feel his touch. Her arm seemed numb and she was almost beyond caring. I'm freezing, she thought. It's a good joke on Koyner. He can't kill us because we'll be dead before he catches us. And then they started across a spot which the wind had swept almost clear of snow, and the horse stepped into a rock crevice and fell.

Tracy was hardly conscious of being thrown. She fell free, enough snow under her to partly break the force of the fall. She saw the horse struggle to rise, and then sink back and only half knew when Lonnigan knelt on the animal's neck, half heard the wind-dulled report as he put a bullet into its brain.

Lonnigan turned away from the horse and moved as quickly as he could to the girl. He tried to bring her to her feet and she fought him, wanting only to lie there in the feathery whiteness and sleep.

He slapped her chilled face. He forced her to walk, propelling her in a circle for several minutes. Then he let her settle back into the snow and, drawing his knife, went back to the horse. He cut the saddle girth and freed the blanket underneath, and then he opened the big belly with slashing strokes, cleaning it and leaving the stomach cavity open and gaping. He spread out the saddle blanket and, picking Tracy up, rolled her in it. He worked doggedly, slowly, as if there were lapses of seconds between the time his brain originated a thought and his stiffened arms responded.

Then he thrust the blanket-wrapped girl into the horse and, using his hat, scooped snow over her to hold in what heat remained. At last he straightened, looking at the snowy mound, realizing that he had done all that was possible.

Tracy's gun had fallen as he rolled her over. He stooped and picked it up, staring down at it for a long moment as if he had never seen a gun before. Then, still carrying it in his gloved hand, he started to backtrack, following the trail that their horse had broken only a few short minutes before.

He moved stiffly, but the wind was now at his back and the driving snow no longer pushed blindingly against his face. He could not see far, but he could see better than the riders coming into the wind. This was his only chance. It gave him a momentary break against his pursuers.

The tracks the horse had made were already drifting over, already filling in, but they were still easy to follow and sooner or later Koyner and his men would come this way. The knowledge kept Lonnigan awake. It kept him on his feet. His first impulse had been to lie down beside Tracy, to wrap the blanket about both of them and wedge as close to the dead animal as they could, but that would profit them nothing if Koyner's men found them.

His idea now was to get as far from Tracy as possible, to make his stand at such a distance that if they killed him, Koyner might not discover the girl, that she might by some miracle live through the storm and find her way safely off the snowy table land.

He sloughed on, his feet dragging tiredly through the heavy snow, forcing himself forward until he reached one of the rocky buttes which rose from the land sharply, a wind-cut pillar of stone.

Here he rested, crouched in the lee of the sharp face, sheltered from the wind, facing in the direction from which Koyner's men would come. He waited, hoping that they would not be delayed, knowing that the cold was eating into his muscles, dulling his reflexes . . . and then his staring eyes picked up the dim shape of Jocko Halleran as it emerged like a shadow out of the blanket of the storm.

He waited, knowing that Halleran would not see him. His clothes were so powdered that he blended perfectly into the outline of the snow-covered rock, and the full force of the blizzard was cutting directly into Halleran's face.

There was no chivalry in Lonnigan now, only a desperate resolve. He knew that his and Tracy's lives depended on his action in the next few seconds.

He steadied the gun he had taken from Tracy, wishing that it had been a rifle, that he would not have the possibility of missing. He waited until it seemed that he could almost feel the breath of Halleran's blowing animal, waited until he could almost reach out and touch the snow-encrusted figure, then he calmly shot Halleran out of the saddle.

And even as he squeezed the trigger he jumped forward and caught the bridle rein of the horse before the man fell. He needed that horse, he had to have that horse, and his hand was savage as he jerked it around when the animal tried to rear.

By main strength he dragged it into the shelter of the butte and lifted himself into the saddle. Lonnigan was a born horseman. He never felt as easy walking as he did on a horse's back, nor as confident. It did something to him to feel the leather between his knees, brought new life to his numb body, new keenness to his storm-dulled brain.

Koyner was less than a dozen feet behind Halleran, yet he did not see clearly enough to realize what happened, for the minute. He heard the shot and drew, and then he saw Halleran's saddle empty and a dim figure wrestling the riderless horse around the butte.

He fired, but he was hampered in pulling his gun by

the cold and the gloves he wore. The night all around him broke into sound as the riders on each flank shouted their startled questions, and began to close up, but they were too slow, for Lonnigan jumped his captured horse around the small butte and was between them, a whitened ghost, helped by the wind at his back which lent added speed to his faltering horse.

A rider loomed out of the white night as Lonnigan went past and Lonnigan fired, the muzzle of his gun not five feet from the man's side. He had a glimpse of the storm-reddened face; he saw the man's hands go up, saw him pitch forward and then he was past, losing him almost at once in the whipping flakes.

He was through their line, for the moment in the clear. Had he been alone on the table he would have ridden for the Junction trail, but there was Tracy. He checked his mount's wild lunges, bringing it unwillingly around. The shouts behind him had died, cut off by the sound of his shot, and nothing broke the persistent howling of the wind, and then, off to his left a gun spat, there was a cry, a curse, and a man's agonized shout.

"Watch what you're shooting at!"

Lonnigan's frozen lips twisted into a stiff grin of amusement. The outlaws were disorganized, shooting at each other, spooked by the knowledge that he was lurking somewhere in the curtain of the storm. And then Koyner's steadying voice.

"You fools! Form a line and ride him down. He's behind us."

Lonnigan did not wait. He drove his spurs against the horse's heaving flanks and headed directly for the sound of Koyner's voice. He was on top of them before they realized that he was not riding away.

He could have knocked over three or four, but he held his fire until he was certain which was Koyner, then pushed straight at the outlaw, firing until the hammer clicked on an empty cartridge. He flung the gun away and pulled his own free of the holster, but Koyner was already dead. Lonnigan's first shot had taken him directly in the forehead. He was already falling when the other bullets struck his swaying body.

Lonnigan's horse plunged into Koyner's as the outlaw fell, slipped and bolted off to the right, scattering the other riders with its headlong plunge. Before him out of the storm loomed another horse, and Lonnigan swerved around trying to avoid a collision. The action saved his life, for one of the men he had just ridden through twisted and fired as he turned. The bullet missed Lonnigan by inches and hit the horse that he had avoided.

It reared, screaming, turning, and as it turned Lonnigan, who was steadying his gun, held his fire, for with a shock he saw that the rider was Kate Jacoby.

He had no time to think about her, to wonder what she was doing here. The girl had somehow managed to keep her seat and the horse did not fall. Instead, maddened with pain, it cut off to the left, racing ahead of Lonnigan as he rode away.

Behind him a dozen shots splattered in the darkness, but presently both he and the girl were lost to the outlaws' sight, and even the sound of their shouts died against the rushing wind.

It was obvious that Kate's horse was out of control and, once clear of the fight, Lonnigan tried to catch it, but, push as he might, he failed to gain on the frightened animal.

Kate had not lost her head and she stayed with the runaway, fighting it doggedly. But she was stiff from cold and her arms lacked the necessary strength to check the pain-crazed beast.

The ride seemed to last an incredible length of time. In reality it must have been measured in minutes only and it came to an end with startling suddenness, for the horse tried to check itself. Then with a horrified, half-smothered cry from Kate, both she and the horse vanished as if she had been swallowed up by the storm.

Lonnigan reined in hard, barely checking his own forward progress before the edge of the table loomed under his horse's nose. The animal shied away, and Lonnigan swung stiffly out of the saddle, moving laboriously in the heavy snow, his bridle hooked over his arm, until he could look cautiously down the sheer drop of the rimrock.

Below him the granite face fell into nothingness. He could see only the boiling clouds of eddying snow and he turned away, shaken so badly that it was minutes before he could remount.

Finally he swung back into the saddle and retraced his way along the tracks that his and Kate's horses had made.

He wasted no time and no regret for Kate. He rode cautiously, trying to keep alert, his gun ready, for Koy-

154

ner's remaining men might be following this trail. But he had neither seen nor heard anyone by the time he reached Koyner's snow-mantled body. He halted, trying to pierce the curtain around him.

The snow was badly trampled and he widened his circle, finally finding what he sought—the broad track that was the outlaws' trail swinging off to the right. For an instant he sat staring down at the sign, not certain, but guessing that they had given up their hunt for him and were quartering across to pick up the Junction trail, that with Koyner dead they were pulling out, for without Koyner they would not know what to do with the stolen silk.

It did not surprise him. Without a leader strong enough to hold them together the band would break apart, splitting into smaller groups which would go their own lawless way. He had, single-handedly, destroyed them, but he felt no lift of elation. He was too bone-tired, too chilled, to feel anything except a nagging worry about Tracy.

He turned back to the butte from which he had started the fight and managed to pick up the snowed-in tracks which led out across the table to the dead horse.

The storm was increasing its fury, lashing against him, tearing at his coat and at the neck scarf which he wore pulled up across his mouth, as if it were making one last desperate attempt to keep them from escaping its violence.

Without the trail he never would have found her, but just as he had begun to believe that he must through some error have got turned around in the storm and followed the wrong trail, he came upon the mound of snow which marked the dead horse.

He dismounted and scooped the snow away. The girl was asleep, still wrapped in the blanket and he was relieved to find some warmth in her hands and cheeks. He left her wrapped in the blanket after he had shaken her awake and she shivered convulsively, clinging to him in sudden desperation.

"It's all right," he said, lifting her into the saddle. "It's all right. They're gone. We're going back."

He urged the horse ahead and followed close behind, the wind at their backs. When they reached the rock where Koyner had died he spoke to Tracy and got no answer, then concluded that she was asleep in the saddle. He pulled her to the ground, shaking her and then forcing her to walk. He led the horse, afraid to let it go since he

155

doubted that his own strength was sufficient to carry them back off the table.

But somehow they made it. The wind at their backs helped, and they followed the tracks directly to the lip of the canyon above the Claflin headframe.

There he released the horse but, as it feared being alone in the storm, it followed them as they came slipping and sliding down the canyon side to the old buildings of the mine.

Lonnigan halted fifty feet above the shaft house and left the girl to creep forward, holding his gun ready. But the place was deserted and Tracy came down to join him, her slight figure so snow-covered that she looked like a snow woman. Lonnigan led her into the shaft house and back into the mouth of the dark tunnel.

There was an old axe in one corner of the shaft house. He used it to splinter the dry boards of the floor and built a fire in the tunnel mouth. Then he knelt and stripped the boots from Tracy's small feet. Afterwards he carried in snow and buried them in it.

Tracy cried out sharply from the burning pain as he chafed circulation back into her legs, then into her hands and cheeks. Afterwards he again wrapped the saddle blanket about her and pulled off his own boots.

His own feet were white and waxlike. He wanted to lie down and sleep, but he didn't dare yet. He brought in snow and forced himself to rub his feet vigorously. He looked up to find that Tracy was watching him, her green eyes looking enormous in the pinched whiteness of her face.

"You," she said, "are kind of unbelievable."

He managed somewhere to find an embarrassed grin. "Still using big words."

"I am an individual who almost always speaks my mind. You know that there is practically nothing you haven't done tonight except one thing."

"What's that?"

"You should have kissed me," she told him. "Heroes generally always kiss girls right after they finally manage to save their lives."

He started to grin again, then saw that there was one large tear squeezing its way out of Tracy's right eye.

"Why, honey." He took her in his arms, blanket and all, and kissed her. Tracy managed to get one small arm free and crooked it convulsively around his neck. He kissed her again. "It's all right," he said. "It's all right. There's nothing to cry about."

"I am absolutely not crying," Tracy protested in a quivering tone, and proceeded to burst into tears. Afterwards she went to sleep, still cradled in his arms. He sat thus, afraid to move, afraid of disturbing her until his arms cramped so badly that he was forced to lay her down. She stirred, smiling in her sleep, but she did not wake.

THIRTY-SEVEN

DAN GOODHUE was with the rescue party which struggled up through the deep snow that blanketed the canyon slope. It was nearly noon and Lonnigan and the girl were hungry, but all right.

Bullock himself was in charge of the party, having ridden into the Junction on horseback with a deputy marshal from Clear Water. They had brought twenty-five heavily-armed men with them, and they were looking for blood.

At the Junction they had found the deserted Silk Express and after talking to Goodhue they had loaded their horses aboard the train and fought their way up through the deep snow to the bridge site. At the bridge site they had fanned out, and it was only the smoke from Lonnigan's fire that had brought them to the Claflin Mine, for although it had stopped snowing, the wagon tracks left by the ore carts had already been obliterated.

Lonnigan heard them coming and stepped out, carrying his gun, then holstered it when he recognized Bullock's bulk and stepped down to where they had halted their horses in the lee of the old mill.

"The silk is safe," he said. "They blew down the wall filling the ore chute, but I know exactly where to dig."

Bullock wasted no time. He sent one rider back to the bridge site with orders for the engineer to return to the Junction and pick up the whole labor crew. Two men he dispatched toward Jacoby's mines to requisition all the ore carts and wagons possible. The rest of the party he led below ground where they attacked the splintered rock with their hands.

Lonnigan saw Tracy talking to Goodhue in the corner and walked toward them. The day agent's freckles stood out like brown blotches against his thin face.

"Tracy just told me about Kate." His tone was low, without emotion.

Lonnigan looked at the girl, and then at Goodhue. "I'll show you where she fell," he offered. "The way I make it, it couldn't have been much more than two miles north of here."

Goodhue shook his head, strangely embarrassed. "If you'll just tell me where to look . . . I'd rather go alone. There was never anything I could do for her alive. I'd like to remember that I was the one to do something now."

Lonnigan led him outside and pointed out the distant rimrock. "Somewhere along the foot of that," he said, and watched Goodhue ride away, leading an extra horse. Then he turned and came back up to the shaft house. Tracy was in the doorway.

"It must be terrible for him," Tracy said softly. "He stayed at the Junction because of her. He knew that she was mixed up with Koyner and never mentioned it to anyone, and he does not parade his grief."

Looking at her, Lonnigan thought that she did not parade her grief either. She had not mentioned her father's death since leaving the station, nor would she. And Lonnigan realized that there was nothing he could do to help her. It was something that Tracy must fight out alone. It ran too deep. It was beyond words so that he knew unconsciously that she would never discuss it with anyone, not even with him.

Before he could answer her Bullock appeared, climbing out of the shaft, followed by Earnest. "We'll have the silk out by the time they get back with the wagons." He was thinking aloud. "If they don't find wagons, we'll sling the bales on the horses and pack out down to the train. The silk will be moving east by evening."

Earnest grunted. "And how do you plan to get it past the Devil's Cut? Remember the bridge is gone."

Bullock was not dismayed. "We'll pack it across and send it into Clear Water on the work train." He turned to Lonnigan. "One thing more, you two. Not one word of the holdup."

Both Tracy and Lonnigan stared at him.

"There wasn't a holdup," he told them. "Bad publicity —give other hard cases ideas. We had a blizzard and a bridge went out."

"You'll never get away with it," Earnest told him. "Too many people know. I'll bet you the news is out within the week."

"Bet me, huh?" Bullock looked at him. "Reminds me— you owe me a bet now. Lonnigan didn't quit. Lonnigan's still here." He looked at Lonnigan, and said with feigned callousness. "Say, why aren't you down in the tunnel, helping move that silk?"

Lonnigan looked at him. He was bone-tired. He felt he had done his part. He started to protest, then turned toward the tunnel without speaking, but Tracy stopped him.

"You," she told Bullock, "are an utter, miserable slave driver. He is not going to carry that silk. He saved it for you, and he almost got killed, and he nearly froze, and that's all the thanks he gets. Well, keep your old railroad. We wouldn't work for you anyway."

Bullock's heavy eyebrows went up quizzically. "We?"

Tracy started to blush, but she stuck by her guns. "Lonnigan isn't going to work for you."

"Yes he is," said Bullock, "but not at a way station. A way station is no place for a married operator. You'll have to bring him into Clear Water, Earnest."

Earnest's mind did not work as fast as Bullock's. "I didn't even know that he was married."

"He will be," said Bullock. "He'll be married within the week or I miss my guess. In fact, I'll bet you on it. But you'd better not bet with me. You never, never win."